BAKWAS

N. GOSNEY

March 2016

To Pam & Darren
Here's to things
that go bump in the night!

Natalie Gosney

First published in Great Britain in 2016 by N. Gosney

The Wolf Born Saga™
The Wolf Born Saga Origins™

Copyright © 2015 N. Gosney

Bakwas Copyright © 2016 N. Gosney

ISBN : 978-0-9575273-4-8

Layout and Typesetting by Philip Gosney
Cover Illustration by Philip Gosney

Werewolf Font by Lettering Delights
www.letteringdelights.com

Bakwas Poem

Oh little child don't wander there, beneath the darkened forest trees.
For he is lurking, watching, waiting; steer clear lest it be you he sees.
At first you may not think him fierce, with gentle voice and soothing ways.
Not revealing that his soul is blacker than the darkest days.

You haven't listened little child, not heeded what your parents told.
Naively thinking that the worst may be a spanking or a scold.
You meet a man, as lost you walk, confused at where you ought to roam.
"Just come along with me my dear, I'll ensure you're safely home."

This kindly stranger offers berries "Come now child, just have a taste.
I can see you must be hungry. Do not let them go to waste."
Trying to entice your senses; fragrant fruits so sweet and rare.
Like a worm to tempt the fishes or a hunter's rabbit snare.

Even if his lies don't fool you, you're his goal; there's no escape.
His eyes will change to demon red with jagged teeth in mouth agape.
The King of Ghosts his name is known; 'Bakwas' whispered through the years.
Taking children to his lover; parents left with plaintive tears.

Your screams are just an echo now, dragged to realms of deathly cries.
Delivered to a monstrous creature; soon to meet your own demise.
Woman of grotesque proportions; dines on human flesh and skin.
Putrid ogre of the forest, tainted by her spirit's sin.

So little child don't wander there, beneath the darkened forest trees.
For he is lurking, watching, waiting; steer clear lest it be you he sees.

- N. Gosney

In loving memory of my dear aunt.
Always in my heart.

Marjana Watling
1950-2015

Contents

—

CHAPTER ONE

Clouds swayed back and forth with a vigorous erratic motion in the blue sky. Richard laughed with delight as he swung, perching on a tyre which was tied to a tree with a strong piece of rope. To his right he noticed the old slide which sat alongside the tree. It was starting to rust, but he didn't care. He knew how exciting it was to stand at the top, feeling like the king of the world, then to whizz dizzily down to the bottom with the wind rushing through his hair. For now however, he was having fun swinging. He closed his eyes and leant backwards in the tyre, clinging tightly to the rope. He kicked his legs back and forth rhythmically, and felt himself flying wildly through the air. 'I'm a bird', he thought in delight, opening his mouth and allowing the warm breeze to hit his face, which proved a welcome relief from the hot sun. His head was dizzy from the rocking motion. He opened his eyes again with his head tilted upwards so the fluffy clouds in the blue sky once again see-sawed back and forth before his eyes. Finally he pulled himself up and dug the toe of his shoe into the chipped wooden bark beneath his feet, causing the tyre to slow down. Richard leapt from it before even coming to a complete stop. He misjudged his jump though, and landed on his back with a thud. 'Ouch', he thought, fighting back the urge to cry. 'I'm not a baby', he inwardly told himself. 'I'm nearly nine. Only babies cry when they fall down.' Gingerly, he rolled over and pushed himself to his feet, bending down to examine the new deep scratch on the back of his leg. 'I'll show my friends at school tomorrow', he thought with pride. A scratch or bruise was always cause for celebration, and if someone had the misfortune of suffering an injury which may lead to a permanent scar, at least they could revel in the knowledge that they'd be admired by their peers as consolation.

A cold wind tickled the back of his neck and he shivered, straightening back up and forgetting about his leg. It had suddenly grown darker, and upon glancing above him, Richard realised the sky was now grey and overcast, a contrast with the lovely sunshine he had been enjoying. 'I'd better get home before it rains', he thought, his button-down blue checked shirt offering little warmth from the suddenly bracing weather. He set off back through the forest the way he had come. His parents didn't mind him coming to the 'playground-den', as he and his friends called it. They'd made it themselves with a tyre from a junk yard and an old slide from his best friend Thomas' garage. Sometimes Richard would meet his friends there and they'd eat a picnic together, but today nobody else had shown up, though Richard didn't know why. He jumped with ease over a fallen log and continued through the trees. He wasn't paying much attention to where he was going though, as his thoughts were full of school, and of what he planned to ask his parents to buy him for his birthday, so when he next looked up he was surprised to find he had no idea where he was.

'This doesn't look right', he thought worriedly. Richard knew his way home like the back of his hand and he was unaccustomed to being in unfamiliar territory. 'Where am I?' He turned and walked back in the direction he had come from but still everything appeared strange; he didn't recognise anything. The trees were bent into unusual shapes, and Richard bit his lip in frustration. 'I have to get home', he thought, feeling his heartbeat racing. In a panic, he pushed through some bushes hoping he might find something familiar behind them, but discovered he had stumbled into another strange clearing. "I'm lost!" he wailed, bursting into tears, not even caring that he was blubbering.

"Lost?" A man's voice echoed through the trees, making Richard jump with fright. He frantically looked about for the owner of the voice.

"You're not lost, child...not with me here. I can take you home." The voice continued to echo, finally stopping behind Richard, who turned sharply, instantly alert.

A man who appeared a little dishevelled stood before him.

His hair was around shoulder-length and scraggly. He wore free-flowing tatty robes, like the hippies Richard had seen so often. 'He looks a bit like John Lennon without any glasses', thought the boy. 'I wonder if he's from the commune mommy and daddy have told me to stay away from.' "You don't know where I live, mister", said Richard, wiping the back of his hand over his eyes and sniffing loudly, embarrassed at having been seen crying. "Are you even from the same town as me? I've never seen you before."

"Of course I am!" said the man with enthusiasm, beaming brightly at the boy. "I know your parents pretty well. I can *easily* get you out of this situation you've found yourself in."

Richard smiled. "Okay, great, that's nice of you; thanks mister." An unpleasant knot in the pit of his stomach told him not to drop his guard, but he dismissed the sensation.

"Come on," said the man, "let's get you home". He held out his hand to Richard who took it willingly, eager to get out of this strange part of the forest. "Before we go, how about a bite to eat?" suggested the man. "You look hungry, and these berries are delicious." He put his other hand in-between the folds of his robes, and when he brought it out again he was brandishing a small handful of ripe purple-blue berries.

"They do look nice", agreed the boy. "What kind are they? Blueberries?"

"A type of Saskatoon berry", replied the man, still smiling. "These ones are extra special and sweet though. Here, try one." He offered the fruit to Richard, who cautiously took one and popped it into his mouth.

"Wow, this is yummy", said the boy, savouring the sweet nutty flavour on his tongue. He swallowed the berry and was about to ask for another, when a strange whispering sound began to echo through the forest. Out of the corner of his eye he thought he saw a shadow, but when he flicked his head in that direction, there wasn't anything there. "Who's that?" he whispered in a fright, tightening his grip of the man's hand. "What's happening?"

The man began to laugh. It was a hollow mirthless sound, which gradually deepened in tone as he flung back his head, until his voice sounded demonic. The whispers all around the boy grew louder and louder, drowning out the laughter. As Richard stared at him in terror, he found it difficult to make out the man's features, and realised with a fright that everything was growing darker. The blackness closed in like a heavy cape, thick and oppressive, until he was entirely plunged into an empty space devoid of all light, and the man had seemingly gone. In a panic, Richard began to run, but he hadn't gone further than a few steps before his foot caught something and he fell hard onto his face. Something sharp dug into his leg as he crashed to the ground, letting out an involuntary cry of pain. Inching forward on his hands and knees, he tried to feel his way, but the whispers and voices echoed around him, terrifying and eerie. He had no idea where he was going. Haltingly, he staggered to his feet and continued on, his arms outstretched so his hands could feel for obstacles that might be blocking his path. He was too petrified to even call out for help, yet Richard knew he had to get out of the forest. The darkness was so intense he felt as though he had gone blind.

After fumbling his way through the trees for some time, trying to drown out the sound of the whispers by humming loudly and tunelessly, tears pouring down his cheeks, he saw something which ignited a tiny spark of hope. 'A light', he thought, squinting to get a better look. He wondered if it was just his imagination; if wishful thinking had produced the light as a mirage to torment him, but the further he walked the brighter it became, so he knew he wasn't merely imagining it. His heart began to race and he started running in the direction of the light, hoping he wouldn't stumble on his way. 'Maybe I've reached the edge of town', he thought. As he drew closer, the light illuminated the building it came from, and Richard could see it was a cabin standing alone in a forest clearing. The trees around the cabin were hazy, as though not quite in focus.

The whispers were now more like voices shouting, "stay away", "run for your life", "don't go in there", "turn back". They echoed over each other almost confusing what each was saying.

"Leave me alone", he yelled, sobbing. The boy stuck his fingers in his ears and ran out of the trees straight towards the cabin.

He flung himself against the door and tumbled into the rustic room, gasping for air in great rasping gulps. "Help me, please!" he begged, falling to the ground. When he looked up, the sight which met his eyes was unlike anything Richard had ever seen before. A huge monstrous ape-like ogress was sitting at a large wooden table, stuffing the remains of what appeared to be a child's foot into her mouth. The head and upper torso of a small boy was lying on the table, but his intestines had tumbled from his gut and were trailing down to the floor. His legs were missing, with blood oozing from ragged stumps where they had been torn clean off. A wave of nausea rose inside Richard and his eyes stung as they began to water. He sat frozen to the spot for a few seconds, as though time had stood still. Then somehow he managed to muster up all his strength and hauled himself to his feet. The brutish woman lurched out of her chair and roared, a great disgusting roar which hit the boy with a blast of stale hot air. The stench of raw undigested meat lingered on her foul breath. Richard let out a strangled cry of terror and stumbled back, falling out of the still open door. The ogress lunged towards him but he scrambled backwards into a bush as the creature peered through the door. He lay still, holding his breath and his tears, as the monstrous woman stepped out of the doorway and walked over to where he was hiding. Richard thought for certain he had been spotted, and was about to scream when the huge creature turned, roared, and headed in the opposite direction. After what seemed an age, Richard got up and ran into the trees away from the cabin and that terrifying cannibal. On and on he ran without looking back. Even though the darkness began once again to envelop him, he didn't slow down or stop. He thought he saw the shadow of the ogress through the trees, and as he turned to head in a different direction, he was sure he could hear the thudding steps of the monster behind, but this was soon drowned out by the multitude of whispers filling the forest. Finally, when the darkness was so thick Richard felt as though he couldn't breathe, once again he saw a light in the distance. 'Please God let this be the edge of town', he prayed silently, running towards it. His legs ached and his lungs burned in his chest, but he kept going until he neared the source of the light. To his horror he recognised the building; it was the same cabin.

Richard's eyes widened and the hairs rose on the back of his neck. 'I swear I didn't run in a circle', he thought, petrified and confused. 'Why am I back here again?' He turned away and ran this time in another direction, continuing to carve a straight path through the trees until it was once again too dark to see anything. Just as he thought he couldn't run any more, another light shone from up ahead. 'Third time lucky', he told himself inwardly. 'Mom always talks about things being third time lucky.' He cautiously approached the light, only to let out a sob of frustration and fear when he realised somehow he had ended up back at the cabin. "No!" he wept. "No, no, no!" He turned away and began to head in yet another direction, then stopped as a massive figure emerged from the trees in front of him. The ogress spotted him immediately, and charged towards him like a bull, taking huge strides. Richard tried to flee but his exhausted legs couldn't carry him away fast enough, and the monster quickly caught up with him. She reached out her arm, fingers outstretched, as though to grab him. The boy ducked, but the ogress smacked his head hard and he fell to the ground. Everything went black.

When Richard regained consciousness at first he didn't know where he was. He felt himself bobbing up and down, being carried along in something. Tentatively, Richard put out his hands and felt his surroundings. The rough texture of woven wicker confirmed his suspicions. 'I'm in a basket of some sort', he thought, beads of sweat trickling down his forehead. He had no time to wonder where he was being taken; the basket was flung carelessly down and Richard tumbled out. The wooden beams and walls of the building he was in were unmistakeable; he was back in the cabin. Pain flooded his body where it had slammed onto the ground. He blinked furiously, only to recoil in horror as the hideous ogress shoved her face close to his and peered at him. "Boy not eat berries!" she bellowed. Flecks of spit flew from her mouth and landed on Richard's cheeks. She grabbed hold of the boy's face, lifting him off the ground. He shrieked in pain as her massive hand started squeezing his skull. "EAT BERRY!" she roared in a monstrous voice. Roughly she threw him to the floor again, and his small body smashed against the wooden planks.

"Uggghhh", groaned Richard. He was sure he had broken something, but he didn't have time to try and check before a handful of berries was mashed into his face by the ogress' massive hand. A few slid down his throat whole, and he began to splutter. 'I can't breathe', he thought in terror, coughing wildly. Eventually he cleared his airway, and he lay stunned on the floor.

The ogress grabbed Richard's shirt sleeve and yanked him towards the far corner of the room, where a large metal cage was situated against the wall. Wrenching open the door, she threw the boy inside and slammed it shut. "When berries start to work, then I eat you", she growled. As Richard struggled to sit up, a haunting sound from outside the cabin flooded his ears; a child, screaming and crying. "More food arrived", spat the ogress. With that, she lumbered over to the door, pulled it open and ambled out, her basket on her back once again. The door slammed shut as she left the building. In desperation, Richard kicked hard against the cage door. To his astonishment, it flew open; the monster had forgotten to lock it. Wasting no time, he crawled out of the cage, staggered to his feet and limped across the room towards the front door. His hip clicked loudly with every step. He tugged on the handle and the door creaked open. An icy unnatural wind blew into the cabin, and Richard stumbled back a few steps. His heart pounded wildly as claw marks began to gouge themselves into the walls of the cabin, etched by invisible talons. Footsteps thudded across the floor heading towards Richard. He stepped back even further, pressing himself against the outside of the cage. Two glowing red eyes and a mouth full of sharp jagged teeth appeared before him. "Dinner", said the entity, in a deep hollow voice.

Richard yelped in terror and dived back into the cage again, slamming the door shut, and cowered in the far corner of his confinements. The glowing eyes pressed up against the bars, peering in.

CHING, CHING, CHING.

The invisible claws ran across the bars, causing sparks to fly in all directions. Richard wanted to close his eyes but he dared not move. He knew the entity was toying with him. It was only a matter of time before he would die. A whimper from outside the cabin turned out to be his only saving grace. With a growl, the eyes turned away from the cage, and Richard heard the creature's footsteps as it strode towards the front door and left the building.

A bundle of rags on the other side of the cage started to move. Richard jumped. "Oh!" he exclaimed. A sharp pain jolted through his ribs and he winced. A tousled dirty blonde head poked itself out from the rags and looked up at him. It was a girl of around twelve. Her face was filthy as though it hadn't been washed in ages, and her hair was matted. She peered at him curiously.

"Has he gone? Why didn't you turn into a spirit?" she asked. "Did you really eat the berries?"

Richard nodded. "Who are you?" he said. "Where am I? What is this place? What were those monsters?" he stumbled over his questions, the words sticking in his throat.

The girl sighed. "It doesn't really matter who I am", she replied. "That monster you just saw though is Bakwas, King of Ghosts. He lures children here to feed Dzunukwa, his greedy fat wife. That's the ogress you met earlier. You're very brave though. Most kids in your position cry a lot more. The berries didn't work on you, and it's not often that happens. There's something…different about you. What is it?"

"Uh…I don't know", said Richard. "What do you mean?"

The girl peered at him closely. "I'm not sure." She sat back and sighed. "Well, they can't eat you, so I suppose you're stuck in here with me. I'm sorry. You'd better keep yourself hidden while you're in here. The few times we've had children who didn't get affected by the berries, those two monsters made short work of them. Just because you can't be eaten doesn't mean you're safe. The last person to end up in here with me would not keep quiet. They didn't last long. Bakwas tore her to pieces and threw her remains on the fire. So please keep hidden and don't draw attention to us. I don't like it when I am made to clean up their messes; they tear into me and bruise me. One time I thought for certain I was going to die." The girl paused to lift up her ragged top at the back, revealing huge claw marks across her shoulder blades.

"Oh that's awful", gasped Richard. "Why have they not eaten you?"

"I used to be like you, from the real world", said the girl. "I've been here for a long time though. At least, I think it's a long time. It's too hard to tell. They forget about me sometimes if I stay hidden, so I hide here, hoping they won't call me out to clean up the cabin. They don't eat me as I haven't eaten any berries."

Richard looked puzzled. "How did you end up here?"

The girl's expression turned to one of sadness. "It's because of my mama", she replied. "It's a long story. She was a witch."

Richard frowned. "Was?"

The girl looked down and sniffed. "Yes…she was."

Richard didn't know what to say. Instead, he glanced out of the cage bars at the room. It was large, with basic wooden furniture. On the floor next to a huge chair, situated at a dining table, was a gigantic pile of bones. The whole room stank of rotten flesh. "Are… are those…?" he began, looking back at the girl.

She lifted her head and slowly she nodded. "All children."

"Wow." Richard stared at the bones. He couldn't even begin to imagine what it must have been like for the girl, watching the man and that ogre Dzunukwa tearing so many children apart in front of her. "I bet that was disgusting", he remarked.

Richard could almost feel the girl's icy gaze boring into his back. "You have no idea", she said. "It's the stuff of your worst nightmares."

Richard shuddered. 'I've got to get out of here', he thought. Every fibre of his being was screaming at him to run away from this awful place. He pushed open the cage door and climbed out cautiously, keeping one eye on the cabin door. He stood up and turned back, reaching into the cage with outstretched hand. "Come on, let's go!"

The girl looked at him hesitantly, made a move as though to reach for him, then pulled her arm back and shook her head.

"Let's go, let's go!" repeated Richard, glancing back at the closed cabin door. The girl took one small shuffle forwards, then stopped. Richard stared at her in confusion. "What's the matter?" he asked.

"I...I can't leave."

"Why not?"

"I...I dare not. If they come back and see me out of the cage without their permission, who knows what they may do to me."

"But we can get out of here!" insisted Richard animatedly. "Let's run away."

The girl paused and looked hard at Richard. "It's pointless you trying to run. Even if you leave the cabin, it wouldn't matter which way you go; everything folds back in on itself. You'd always find that you're heading back towards the cabin. They'd eventually find you anyway; they always find runaways. You can't hide forever."

Richard stared at the girl in horror. "Is there nothing we can do?"

The girl slumped her shoulders. "I've tried every spell I could find in my mama's book. Anything to get out of this place. They don't work; nothing works. For some reason I can't do magic any more - I haven't been able to since the day she died."

"What book?" asked Richard.

"It was lying on the ground next to her", said the girl, her voice beginning to tremble. "It's only small, but it's full of spells, journal entries...all sorts of things; I could tell they're written by her hand. I had it in my pocket when I was brought here."

"Where is it then?" asked Richard. "Show me."

"Bakwas and Dzunukwa didn't find it on me at first, but I didn't want to take any chances. The first time they left me alone to clean the house, I hid it." She paused and bit her lip. "It's...in the other room." She pointed with one shaky finger to a door on the far side of the living room.

"Should I get it?" asked Richard fearfully. He gulped. "What else is in the other room?"

The girl's eyes widened, and she stared at Richard. "Their children", she whispered. "They're asleep now."

She had spoken so quietly that Richard wasn't sure he'd heard her correctly. "Ch...children?" he repeated.

The girl nodded.

"Those monsters are parents?" asked Richard, his eyebrows rising. "But...they *eat* children."

"These are not like proper children", whispered the girl.

Richard gulped. Again he looked anxiously at the door leading to the other room. It seemed so far away, yet so near at the same time. His body twitched to flee from the cabin and run into the forest, but he knew it would be futile. Staying in the cage was out of the question. That left only one further option, but Richard couldn't move. "I..." he began. Then he closed his eyes, inhaled sharply, and took one small step in the direction of the bedroom door.

The girl let out a tiny gasp. "Don't", she warned.

Two tears trickled out from under Richard's eyelids. "I can't stay here", he said. "Where is the book?"

"It's under a floorboard between one of the cribs and the window", replied the girl. "The crib on the left."

Richard opened his eyes and took another step. His knees almost buckled and he dug his fingernails into the palm of his hands, clenching his fists tightly, trying to summon up a shred of courage. He took another step, then another, and another. The floorboards creaked, and Richard dared not to even breathe. 'Just keep moving', he told himself, fearing that if he halted he would be unable to start walking again. With every step his heart beat faster and louder; he thought it would burst out of his chest. Finally he stopped in front of the door, so close he just needed to lift his hand and push it. Richard stood motionless, staring at the wood, sweat dripping from his forehead.

"Don't", whispered the girl from the cage.

Richard clamped his lips together firmly. He didn't want to cry out. 'Be brave', he told himself. 'Be brave.' With one shaky finger outstretched, he reached out and touched the door. 'Be brave.'

He pushed. The door slowly creaked open.

CHAPTER TWO

Upon entering the room, Richard was plunged into darkness. It didn't take long for his eyes to adjust to their surroundings. Quickly he closed the door behind him, not wanting the light to wake the sleeping children. 'If that's even what I should call them', he thought. He cast his gaze around the room. Two grossly oversized makeshift wooden cribs were pushed up against each wall to the sides of the room. Ahead of him was a window, but it didn't allow much light in. Richard looked back at the cribs. Bent nails stuck out at all angles from them, and sharp splinters of wood protruded dangerously from the twisted looking furniture. Loud inhuman snores emanated from them. Richard cringed. 'I can't do this', he thought. Every bone in his body wanted to run out of the room and back to the girl. Even the cage seemed more appealing than trying to cross this dark bedroom. Still he urged himself onwards.

'Two cribs. One on the left, and one on the right', he thought, remembering what the girl had told him. 'I need the left one.' He tiptoed towards the crib, treading lightly. 'Nearly there', he thought. He wished the girl were with him. It might have given him courage to have someone by his side, but he had to do this alone. More snoring echoed around the room; Richard didn't want to see what kind of creatures were filling those cribs. Then it happened.

CREAK.

Richard had stepped on a slightly loose floorboard. 'Oh no!' he thought in a panic, praying the children hadn't heard it. He dropped to the floor in desperation, and began to crawl towards where he hoped the book might be hidden.

CREAK. CREAK. CREAK.

Every plank he crawled across let out a noise so loud it could have woken the dead, or so it seemed to Richard. A strangled cry erupted from the crib adjacent to him, which started to rock violently.

'It's awake. Oh no it's awake', thought Richard, his heart in his mouth. He looked over at the floor between the crib and the window. Already he could see which of the floorboards he needed to reach. One was tilted upwards slightly, as though it had been disturbed. 'It's definitely that one', he thought.

The crib continued to lurch, propelled by the motions of the creature within. To Richard's horror, he realised the rickety bed was inching closer to the window. 'No! No, no, no!' he silently prayed. It was no use. The crib rocked straight over the floorboard plank Richard needed to access, pinning it down and making it impossible to lift. The rocking slowed and eventually stopped, with the child having apparently fallen back to sleep.

Richard felt like crying. A sob threatened to escape from him, and he had to press his lips together to avoid making a sound. He briefly considered giving up, but despite his tender age his stubborn streak was strong, and he shook his head resolutely. He stuck out a hand and took hold of one of the large bent-looking rockers, slowly jiggling it up and down to sway the crib. 'If I can get it off this floorboard, I can get to the book', he thought.

Up and down, up and down, Richard rocked the crib, pushing it gently with each rock, until at last it was off the floorboard plank. He didn't waste a moment. He clenched his fingertips around the plank, which lifted up when he pulled, revealing a small brown leather book below. It had a long leather belt which wrapped around the journal to keep it closed. He tried to pull it up, but the book wedged in the opening. Richard tugged hard and it came free, popping out like a cork from a bottle. Richard's arm flew back and his elbow smashed against the side of the crib. A squeal sounded out and the crib once again began to shake and rock. Realising he would be wasting time if he put the floorboard back into place, Richard dived to his feet and began to race for the door but a loud crash behind him caused him to jump and look back. One of the crib's rockers had wedged into the hole where the floorboard had been, sending the jerking crib toppling to the ground. Richard stepped backwards in a panic, his back pressing against something. Then he screamed as a long ogre-like arm grabbed him from behind. Peering back he realised he was against the other crib, and the second creature was now leaning out, gripping Richard tightly. It grunted loudly, making a similar sound to Dzunukwa. Richard tried to squirm away, but his assailant was strong and he couldn't free himself. "Get off me!" sobbed Richard. From the upturned crib, a pile of ragged blankets which had been deposited on the floor began to move. A black creature, almost demonic in appearance, started to drag itself along on its belly towards Richard. Using its talons to grip between the floorboards, it pulled its body across the floor. A terrifying smile on the creature's face reached from ear to ear, revealing an almost unending set of razor sharp teeth. With its mouth slightly parted, a long snake-like tongue emerged, whipping around wildly and running across its top row of teeth. Its eyes glowed bright red, just as Bakwas' had done, and the creature inched towards the boy.

"NO!" screamed Richard. He bent his head and bit the arm which was holding him tightly. The child roared and loosened its grip, just enough for Richard to wriggle away from it. He dived for the door, but the demonic creature on the ground stretched out its hand and grabbed his foot. Its talons sank easily through the material of Richard's footwear. He fell heavily and kicked out behind him, his foot squarely making contact with the monster's face, losing his shoe in the process. The creature began to cry; an unearthly wail that sounded as though it had been formed in the pit of hell. Somewhere between a screech and a deep unsettling moan, the noise made Richard's blood run cold. He scrambled to his feet and flung himself at the door. He yanked it open, threw himself out, and slammed it shut behind him. He could hear clawing and scratching at the door which he backed away from in terror, panting hard.

"Are you alright?" cried the girl, from the relative safety of the cage.

Richard ran over to her, leaving the terrible noises of the

bedroom behind him. He crawled through the cage opening and closed the door just in time, for at that moment Dzunukwa barged into the living room, her basket on her back. The girl let out a squeak and huddled under the rags in the cage. "Get down", she hissed.

The screeches and roars from the bedroom were still ongoing, and Dzunukwa let out a grunt as she heard the commotion her children were making. She threw the basket to the ground, and lurched into the bedroom to attend to her demonic offspring. The basket began to shake. As Richard watched, the lid popped open and out crawled a dishevelled frightened looking face that Richard recognised so well.

"Thomas!" called Richard. Never before had he been more relieved to see his best friend. Something seemed wrong though; Thomas didn't appear quite in focus. He was slightly hazy in appearance.

The boy's gaze settled on Richard. "What are you doing here?" he asked, racing over to the cage. "Where are we? How did you get here? What's that giant thing that carried me?"

Richard didn't answer his friend's questions. There was something more important he needed to ascertain. "Did you eat the berries?" he asked.

Thomas blinked in astonishment. "What?"

"It's really important. Did you eat the berries?"

"Um…yes. So what? What are we doing here? Where are we?"

Richard felt his stomach flip over. 'If Thomas has eaten the berries, that means…' "Run!" he hissed desperately at Thomas. "Get out of here! They're going to eat you!"

Thomas' eyes widened and all colour drained from his face. He didn't stop to ask any more questions, but turned and raced to the front door. He was mere steps away from it when it swung open before him, and with a whoosh some sort of invisible entity whirled into the cabin. Thomas raised his arms and shrieked, but four huge slashes sliced into them from invisible claws. For a split second Richard thought his friend had merely been cut as the blood trickled out, but almost immediately Thomas' arms thudded to the floor. Blood poured from his stumps and began to pool over the floorboards. He let out an ear splitting scream of pain and terror, as glowing red eyes and large sharp teeth appeared in front of him.

"Dinner", it said, in a deep voice which made Richard's blood run cold.

As Richard watched, his eyes as wide as saucers, four patches of blood appeared in Thomas' back, as though a pitch fork had been run through him. He fell to the floor gasping for breath, and the entity bent down and sank its teeth into Thomas' gut, ripping out his intestines. It was like a piranha eating its prey. Richard recoiled in horror and vomited onto the ground. He felt something tugging at his arm, and turned to see the girl. She looked concerned, and stared into his eyes earnestly. "Look away", she whispered. "Did you get the book?"

Richard couldn't tear his gaze away from what was happening to his friend. Tears flowed freely down his cheeks, and his mouth tasted of the sick he had brought up. The girl tried again, pulling him until he was forced to turn away from the stomach-churning scene in the living room.

"He'll be busy eating for a little while", the girl whispered. "The book, please..."

Richard fumbled in his pocket and pulled out the small brown spell book. He carefully unwound the belt from around it, and lifted the front cover. The pages were yellowish and the handwriting was hard to make out, but he flipped through the pages at random. The disgusting guzzling noises from behind him were ringing through his head and he tried to block them out, but it was no use. "I don't know what to look for", he admitted, flicking through pages of scrawled notes. He paused to look at a crude diagram of what appeared to be a green crystal. "Em...er...on", he read aloud. "What's an emeron?"

"Oh, I have one of those", said the girl. She tugged at something around her neck, and from underneath her ragged top she produced a small pouch. "I found it next to the book not long before Bakwas captured me."

"It's pretty", said Richard. "Do you suppose it's special?"

"I suppose so, but I can't imagine how", replied the girl.

Richard stared at the picture in the book again curiously, before turning the page. "Banishment spell", he read. "What does banishment mean?"

"It means to get rid of something. It sounds like it might be worth a try", said the girl. "If we can banish Bakwas and Dzunukwa, maybe we'll be freed." She tried to keep her expression neutral, but Richard could see from the sparkle in her eyes she was secretly excited. He hadn't seen anything in those eyes until now apart from despair.

"What if..." Richard bit his bottom lip. "What if it doesn't work?" A lump caught in his throat at the thought of never going home again.

The girl squeezed her eyes shut. "Don't say that," she whispered, "it has to". She swallowed hard several times, as though trying to compose herself, then she re-opened her eyes and looked at Richard intently. "You have to do this", she said seriously. "Look, I know you have no natural magic, but we're in the land of the dead, so anything is possible. It's better than trying nothing at all. If it doesn't work, we'll be no worse off than we are now. Besides, there's something different about you, otherwise the berries would have changed you...and they didn't."

"Okay", agreed Richard. He felt sick, and wished fervently that this entire plan didn't depend on him performing a spell when he knew nothing about magic, but he also knew the girl was right, there was no other option. A loud bang behind him made him jump, and he turned around in a hurry to see what had happened. Almost immediately he wished he hadn't. Dzunukwa had come from the bedroom, carrying her two demonic children. In the light of the room it was easier to see what they looked like. One was almost like a younger version of its mother; a small ogre, yet still huge for a toddler. Its ape-like features contorted into a look of gluttonous desire as it saw Thomas' mutilated body lying on the ground. The other was more like its father; a black demonic beast with glowing red eyes and sharp teeth. Dzunukwa placed them on the floor, then sat down beside Bakwas. Strangely Thomas appeared to be still alive. A strangled gurgle was coming from his throat, and his body was twitching uncontrollably. Dzunukwa reached down to the boy's legs and ripped one off. Thomas' gurgle turned into a high pitched shriek as his tendons tore apart. The ogress brought the leg up to her mouth and sank her teeth into it, making appreciative gulping sounds. The two young monsters picked up Thomas' arms, one each, and began munching on them. Thomas' desperate screams pierced through Richard's ears, nearly deafening him. He turned to the girl. "How is he still alive? This is horrible", he sobbed. "Thomas, my friend Thomas. They have to let him go!" He hadn't quite realised how loud he was being until the girl clamped her hand over his mouth.

"Shhhh!" she hissed, the fear in her eyes being obvious. "He ate the berries, so he's ghost food now. That's his spirit, his soul; that's what they're eating. His body died already when he ate the berries. That's what they do; they kill you and turn your spirit into ghost food. Well…they're supposed to. It didn't work on you for some reason."

A growl from across the room made Richard and the girl both jump. Richard immediately looked around to see the demon-like child staring at him, licking its blood-covered lips. "Oh God," he whispered, beginning to tremble, "one of them has seen us".

"It's now or never", said the girl, her voice starting to crack. "You have to try the banishment spell."

Richard swallowed hard, lifted the book, and began to read aloud from it. The words were foreign and complicated to his tongue. It was a language Richard was unfamiliar with; he supposed it was a magical language. The words stuck in his throat as he spoke them, but he forced them out. The infant was dragging itself across the floor, claws digging into the floorboards as it scraped along on its stomach. Richard tried to speed up what he was saying, but he couldn't sound out the pronunciations fast enough. 'Please don't come here', he thought, sweat clinging to his brow. His inward pleadings were in vain though as the creature reached the cage and stuck its chubby arm through the bars. Razor sharp claws swiped at Richard, who leant back as far as he could, trying to put himself out of the child's reach. The girl, in turn, was cowering in the far corner of the cage, her knees up to her chest and her face buried in them, as though she wanted to hide but couldn't quite manage. 'Keep chanting', Richard told himself. He struggled to concentrate on the words; his every instinct focused on staying away from the young monster.

The child pushed harder, and every confidence Richard had previously had in the cage being a safe haven was shattered when the two bars around the creature's arm began to bend slightly. Richard strained against the back of the cage, wishing his cell had more depth to allow him to shuffle even further backwards. With a grunt of frustration, the creature jabbed at Richard's legs, managing to sink its claws into his knee. Richard's first reaction was to scream from the pain now running the length of his leg, but he didn't. He knew he had to keep going with the spell. With gritted teeth and a determination of someone three times his age, he continued to chant. At first there didn't seem to be anything happening, but then Richard became aware of a tiny almost imperceptible change in the room. A breeze was blowing. It was one of those things you dismiss at first. After all, a breeze is not particularly noticeable, but the more he chanted, the stronger this draught became. It caught the attention of Bakwas, who looked up from chewing on Thomas' body. His own form was visible now, black as pitch, just like the child still clinging to Richard's leg. Defiantly, Richard raised his voice, shouting his chant as loudly as possible.

Bakwas' eyes flashed an ever brighter red as he realised what was happening. "Nooooo!" he screamed. In the centre of the room a small black dot appeared, and the vortex now filling the cabin began to rush into it at a great speed. Richard realised it was not a dot, but rather a hole. Bakwas rushed at the cage but was thrown backwards by the force of the air being sucked into abyss. The baby by the cage was flung into the air; its claws tore huge gashes in Richard's leg as it tried to cling to him, but it was no use, its arm bent the bars as it got blown against the side of its father. Richard screamed in pain cupping his wound. The front door of the cabin flew open as the vortex pulled everything towards the hole. The girl shrieked as Dzunukwa was propelled in the direction of the cage.

"Run!" yelled the girl, pushing Richard out of the cage and causing the book to tumble from his grasp, just as Dzunukwa smashed into it, crumpling the bars with her gargantuan frame. The girl hadn't quite managed to get clear of the impact, and hit her head hard against the side of one of the bars. Her body fell to the ground in a heap, completely unconscious. Richard turned back and tried to reach through the battered cage frame to get to her, but it was so crushed it was nearly impossible. He pushed harder; instead of grabbing his friend though, his fingers made contact with the book beside her. He strained a little further but was filled with an excruciating pain in his other shoulder. Bakwas' claws had dug into him, and he was flung away from the cage with tremendous force, book still in hand. Winded, he grabbed hold of a shelf on the far wall. The black dot began to increase in size. The monstrous ogress slid away from the cage and slowly started to move across the floor towards the black hole. She bellowed and roared, digging her talons into the wooden floorboards, fighting against the wind. With a gasp, Richard realised she was trying to head his way. He could feel his own body being sucked towards the black hole as well, and he clung to the shelf in desperation, his legs flying out behind him. Knowing he had to get to the front door, he reached for a wooden beam jutting out from the wall which would have taken him slightly closer to the exit. Before he could move though, something grabbed his foot. He didn't even have to look to know it was Dzunukwa. Her grotesque stench reached his nostrils even before he glanced down at her. With a jolt he shot back and his fingers nearly lost their grip on the shelf. He clung on tight as the huge brute pulled once more, causing the shelf to slowly sag away from the wall as nails became exposed.

"Get off!" screamed Richard, kicking his legs violently. With an almighty crack the shelf came away from the wall altogether, and he shot towards the ogress with it still in his hand. Without a second thought, he swung it around and whacked the brute straight across the face as he tumbled past her. Dzunukwa let out

a roar and her fingers lost their grip on his leg. The whirlwind in
the room grew stronger as the black hole doubled in size. Richard
was flung across the room and smashed against the far wall,
momentarily pinned there by the outer ebb of this unnaturally
destructive force. He watched in horror as the mangled body of his
friend Thomas slid across the floor, leaving a deep red blood smear
on the wood, then was lifted into the air and pulled into the abyss.
"Thomas!" screamed Richard, sobbing wildly. He knew his friend
was dead, but he still hadn't been prepared for that moment of
absolute finality. It was only at that point it hit him he would never
see Thomas again.

Barely even able to see through his tears, Richard felt his body
being picked up once again and bounced around from wall to
wall. Every thud jolted through his body, and he was sure he had
broken several bones. He saw a fuzzy black shape heading towards
him, and a pair of demonic red eyes. Bakwas was clawing his way
along the wall with ease, defying gravity like a spider. Richard
was sure he was about to smash into the monstrous figure, and
he closed his eyes tightly bracing for an impact which he knew
Bakwas would take advantage of. 'Those claws are going to tear
through me', thought Richard, his heart racing. Sure enough the
King of Ghosts reached up to swipe at the boy, but a violent thrust
of air carried the boy over his head. Bakwas bellowed in anger as
Richard bounced against the far wall. He would have ricocheted off
it had he not grabbed hold of a cupboard door which was swinging
back and forth violently in the extreme wind. 'I don't think I can
hold onto this for long', he thought, his fingers slipping. His arms
strained in their sockets, and Richard was sure they were going to
be ripped clean from his body. He summoned up all his strength
and flung his legs onto the kitchen counter below the cupboard he
was clinging to. 'You can do this Richard', he told himself. 'One…
two…three!' As he counted three he let go of the cupboard door
and immediately grabbed the edge of the kitchen counter. He was
now lying on it on his front, arms out above his head, his fingers
tightly gripping the sides of the work surface. His legs were still
being pulled from side to side in the vortex. 'I need to get to the

door', he thought in desperation. He hauled himself forward on his stomach with a grunt, then screamed as the twisted cage flew past his head, dragging the still unconscious girl along with it, straight into the black hole. "NOOOO!" he shrieked. His cry was drowned out though by a horrible bellow of rage and anguish. Out of the corner of his eye he saw the two monstrous toddlers being sucked from their mother's arms and whirling twice around the room amidst squeals and grunts of terror, before disappearing along with most of the furniture, the cage, and the girl into the abyss. Too concerned with her offspring to think of grabbing hold of anything, Dzunukwa appeared to realise too late that her legs were being blown out from underneath her. She scrabbled in vain to get a foothold on something, but fell with a loud crash to the ground before sliding on her back across the floor towards the hole, where she, too, was swallowed up entirely.

Richard lunged himself forward on his belly. He slid off the kitchen worktop and tumbled wildly through the air, just managing to grab the handle of the front door as his bruised body spun around. The force of the wind pulling him towards the black hole yanked the door open as well. He tried to thrust himself out of the cabin, but a sharp pain flooded his thigh and started yanking him backwards. He cried out in agony and looked back, seeing Bakwas clinging to his leg. His red eyes flashed angrily, as his talons penetrated Richard's flesh. He began to clamber up the body of the boy as though scaling a ladder. Richard kicked out and thrashed, but in vain, for he was too terrified of being sucked from the door and blown into the void. Finally Bakwas clung to Richard's back, and his razor sharp teeth sank into the boy's shoulder. A searing pain coursed through Richard's entire body, and he jerked involuntarily with sharp twitching motions. So intense was the sensation that he felt as though he would pass out. Then, just as suddenly as it had started, the pain lessened and he felt the weight shift off his back. He looked around to see the ever enlarging hole sucking the King of Ghosts into its vast empty blackness. The monster's grip on Richard was slipping, and Richard tried to pull forwards, but just as he thought he was going to make it through the door another burning pain engulfed his leg. Bakwas had slipped down his body and was clinging to his calf in an attempt to prevent himself from being pulled into the hole.

Richard screamed in terror and agony; he knew he wouldn't be able to hold onto the door handle for much longer. Violently he kicked out with his free foot, catching Bakwas in the face. The creature's blade-like claws sliced further down his shin as the King of Ghosts finally let go and tumbled head over heels into the darkness. The pain surging through Richard's leg was unbearable, and his grip loosened on the handle. For a moment he was sucked towards the black hole, but was then shoved abruptly through the open door by a strong blast of swirling wind. He shot out of the cabin and was deposited onto the ground, rolling over several times before stopping. With a groan he turned his head back to look at the building which was creaking with the strain of the cataclysmic events occurring within it. Richard's eyes opened wide, as suddenly, with an almighty bang, the entire thing collapsed into itself, sending out a blast of freezing cold wind and a flash of light which felt as though it had burned the back of his retina. He gasped and clamped his eyes shut. 'I'm blind, oh no I'm blind', he thought in a panic.

After a while everything was still and quiet around him. Silence and darkness followed. Richard could hear only the beating of his own heart, and his shallow breath mingled with his soft sobs as he lay almost motionless. For a moment he remained where he was, too petrified to move, but then slowly he sat up. The darkness began to lighten, first to grey; Richard started to see shapes of objects around him. Tall, faceless shadows surrounded him, and at first he was convinced it was Bakwas and Dzunukwa here to capture him again. Then he noticed they weren't moving, and there were far too many to be just two people. Trembling, he pushed against the ground to stand up, and staggered towards one of the objects. Every bone in his body screamed with pain, and blood gushed from his wounded leg. 'It's only a tree', he realised, able to see the figure more clearly now he was closer to it. Soon the whole forest was visible, bathed in daylight filtering through the treetops, and Richard saw to his relief he was back in the real world.

He felt the toe of his shoe kick something, and when he looked down he saw the spell book. "Some use you were!" he cried, hurling the book as far as he could throw. "I'm alive, but Thomas and the girl aren't!" The loneliness and grief which had built up inside his stomach erupted like a volcano. He sank to his knees sobbing, deep gasping heart-felt cries of anguish. "I've left her there, she was banished along with them! She's probably dead! Thomas, oh poor Thomas, I couldn't save him! Look what they did to him!" he wailed. He realised he had to get up and make his way home, but the trauma of what he had been through was more than he could bear. He remained on the dry muddy ground, lying on his side with his knees scrunched up in a foetal position, in pain from the bite on his shoulder and the claw marks cutting through his leg. Blood began to drip where he lay, as he started to weep for Thomas and the girl he hadn't managed to save, and whose name he didn't even know, until he felt cold and weak, and eventually fell asleep.

CHAPTER THREE

Richard's eyes sprang open. It was dark, and for a moment he wondered if he was still in the forest. Then it hit him all at once; he wasn't, in fact, a little boy any longer, but a fully grown man of twenty-five, exactly as he should be. 'Oh my God, what a nightmare!' he thought, groaning as he sat up in bed. His pillow was soaked as though he had been crying, and sweat was pouring from every inch of his body. Beside him was his fiancée, the blankets moving slightly up and down with every breath she took. The dream Richard had just experienced was one of the most realistic he'd ever encountered, and the most harrowing part was that it didn't even feel like a dream; it felt like a discarded memory. 'I wonder if this was a reoccurring dream that I'd forgotten about previously', he thought, shaking his head to try and clear it. Still trembling, he stood up and tentatively made his way into the bathroom to splash water on his face. 'The girl, I swear I've seen her before', he thought. The wind had felt so real, and his heart still jumped every time his mind flicked back to thoughts of Bakwas and Dzunukwa. 'Those are very specific names which couldn't have just be made up in a dream', he realised. With trembling hands he bent down and rolled up the left leg of his pyjamas and examined his ankle. There they were, the marks he had lived with for so long. He pulled the material up further to reveal deep long scars across his thigh. He checked his shoulder, revealing the healed but still visible bites. 'I always assumed these were injuries caused by an animal attack. At least that's what my parents told me when I woke up in hospital. I never remembered what really happened. The doctors told me it was blocked out because of my traumatic experience', he thought. His mind flicked to the baby in his dream that had grabbed his leg through the cage bars, and he remembered Bakwas digging his claws into his calf. 'It has to be a coincidence, doesn't it? It was just an animal, not a monster like that', he reasoned with himself. Richard rubbed his eyes and shook his head. 'Don't be stupid,' he told himself, 'of course it was an animal. I've been through those woods countless times, and never encountered anything like that.'

True he remembered his friend Thomas' disappearance. It wasn't something he could never forget. His face had appeared on milk cartons, but still the boy had never reappeared. Eventually Thomas' parents had moved away from town, hoping to start a new life somewhere else. Nobody ever found out what had happened to Thomas. The notion that he had been eaten by those creatures was a little too much for Richard to take. 'It was only a dream', he told himself. Still it had unnerved him, and he decided the only way to clear his head would be to go out for a brief hunt. It would be good to focus his attention on something else. He emerged from the bathroom and peered through the darkness at his sleeping fiancée on the bed, grateful of his enhanced vision which enabled him to see her clearly. Her blonde hair cascaded over the pillow, and he could tell from her deep breathing she wouldn't wake easily. He sighed. 'How has it come so far without me telling her about myself?' he thought, as he had done a thousand times lately. 'We'll be married in a few weeks and she still doesn't know.'

He ran his fingers through his hair agitatedly. 'I've got to tell her at some point soon. I can't commit her to a life with me without revealing the truth to her. She has no idea what she's getting herself into.' He had never actually intended to get married. As the son of werewolves, this was a secretive life which he had been born into. It was not without its problems though, and he'd always sworn to himself he wouldn't inflict this on anybody else. Sure, the abilities were great; heightened senses, enhanced speed…but the monthly change was utter torture. The first time he'd gone through it shortly after turning thirteen, he'd thought he was going to die. Bones cracking, fingertips and gums bleeding…Richard shook his head to clear his mind of the memory. 'It never gets any easier', he thought bitterly.

Things had taken a sudden turn when he'd met Laura. Blue eyes, blonde hair, and stunning good looks you only tended to see in Penthouse magazine (not that he would ever let on to Laura he still had his old copies of Penthouse stuffed in a box in the basement). Laura wasn't only attractive, she was also intelligent and caring; he had never met anyone like her before. He had to admit the attraction had been instant, and he knew, even as he asked her out for coffee, this was going to be more than just a one night stand. Here they were though, two years later, and he still hadn't worked up the nerve to let her into his deepest secret.

'It's ridiculous that she doesn't even question where I go once a month', he thought, staring at the shadows flitting across the wall as the headlights of a passing car cast their beams through the thin curtain against the window. He didn't personally think his excuses were very plausible. Sometimes he told her he was going out with friends, other times he said he was working late. None of these were particularly valid reasons to be out all night, but if Laura suspected him of infidelity she never showed it. 'I'd never do that to her though', he thought, narrowing his eyes. Sometimes, of course, he considered cheating to be a lesser secret than being a werewolf. At least that was something...normal. Sighing again, he headed for the door. He didn't need to change his clothes; he wouldn't even need his pyjamas soon. He did grab a bag on his way out though. With a brief backwards glance at Laura, he crept outside into the dark.

The night air was cool and the moonlight shone down, casting shadows through the forest leaves. Richard crouched behind a tree; he removed his pyjamas and placed them in his bag which he hid inside a small bush. 'Hopefully this hunt will take my mind off things', he mused, as his body started to ripple and contort. Like a wave which ran through his whole body, he transformed into a large sandy coloured wolf within mere seconds. He sniffed the bracken beneath his feet, lifted his head, and peered into the distance. He always loved his wolf senses; he knew the smell of a rabbit, and his sharp vision cut through the darkness without effort. There, not far ahead, was the animal he sought. 'I've got you now', he thought, as he began to bound at tremendous speed towards the rabbit. Oblivious to his presence, the creature remained stationary.

Richard leapt for the kill, but something hit him from the side causing him to slam into the ground and roll. Jumping up, he noticed the rabbit bolt into the distance, and a large cougar stared him down. 'Oh hell! I don't want any trouble', he thought, not breaking the cougar's gaze. He began to cautiously back away, but before he could run he heard a hiss behind him, followed by a long low growl. 'Not another one', he thought, glancing away to see a second slightly larger cougar approaching slowly from behind. He positioned himself so he could see them both, as they closed in on him.

The pair of cougars circled him, one male and one female, padding softly with their bodies crouched low. He, in turn, tensed his muscles, trying to keep an eye on each of the mountain lions simultaneously, but it was difficult. 'I only wanted to catch a bite to eat, for God's sake', he thought, irritated. 'There aren't usually mountain lions around here. Where the hell did they come from?' There seemed little use to speculate though. These two were here, and they obviously weren't very happy about sharing this hunting spot with Richard. Although, being a werewolf he was significantly larger than the cougars, he was acutely aware he was outnumbered. 'This should be interesting', he thought wryly. He growled and bared his sharp teeth, hoping that would be enough to scare them into backing off, but to no avail. The circling continued. 'Take the goddamned hint', he thought with frustration.

The female cougar snarled viciously. Richard gritted his teeth. 'Okay, well, I can't stay here all night.' Springing into action, he leapt forwards, looking for a way to dive through the gap between the two mountain lions. The male lashed out with its claws as he passed, gashing Richard deeply across his side. 'Son of a...' Richard thought, falling to the ground with a whine. The female bounded towards him, but he jumped to his feet, trying to ignore the searing pain from his wounds. Fluidly, he lunged at the approaching female and clamped his jaws around its leg.

The cougar let out a strangled yelp and tried to shake Richard off, but he held on tightly. 'No you don't, you goddamned creature', he thought, as the cougar brought its other paw up to swat at him. Suddenly a sharp stabbing sensation coursed through his back. He released the female's leg, and uttered something between a growl, a howl, and a whine. He tried to swing around, but was encumbered by the weight of the male cougar on his back pushing him down. 'I'll teach you to bite me', he thought threateningly, wishing he could speak mountain lion. Quickly, he flung himself towards a tree, slamming the cougar into it at full force. The male cougar hissed and spat at him as it fell. That gave Richard a brief moment of opportunity to dive at the injured limping female, which turned to face him just in time for him to sink his teeth into her jugular. She flinched, but he ripped out her throat before she could even react. 'Sorry but it was either you or me', he thought. He didn't like confrontations with other forest animals, and avoided them wherever possible, but sometimes they were unavoidable. The female let out a gurgle and slumped to the ground, blood beginning to pour from her neck and mouth.

"Nizhoni!" screamed a voice from behind Richard.

Startled, he stepped back from the female and turned rapidly to see who had shouted. To his astonishment, the male cougar had disappeared, and in its place stood a naked man, perhaps in his forties. He looked Native American and his jet black hair was long and wild. In one of his hands he held an animal skin. Richard gasped as he realised it was the pelt of a mountain lion.

"Nizhoni!" the man cried again, rushing past Richard and throwing himself on the ground next to the dying female cougar. He put his arm under its head, cradling it. The animal looked at him, blood flowing from its mouth onto the man's arm. Its breathing grew shallow, and it let out a final shudder, before Richard heard its heart stop beating. "Oh no no, Nizhoni, no!" wailed the man in despair. Richard watched in horrified fascination as the cougar's body changed from feline form, to that of a female Native American about his age, mid-twenties. A cougar skin seemed to fall from her body, and it lay on the bracken beside her. The woman's left arm looked badly injured, and Richard realised with a jolt that he had caused the wounds.

'Oh my God!' he thought in disbelief. 'Werecougars? Whoever heard of a werecougar? What the hell is the animal skin for? Oh shit, I've killed someone!" He couldn't move for shock.

The man gently removed his arm from underneath the woman's head, stood up, and turned to face Richard with a dangerous expression. "You filthy dog, you killed Nizhoni", he spat. "You should know better than to anger the leader of a Yee Naaldlooshii tribe.

'What the hell is a Yee Naaldlooshii tribe?' thought Richard, feeling totally confused. 'Does he know I'm a werewolf, or does he think I'm an ordinary wolf?'

"I know you can understand me, dog", the man continued, his expression wild with grief and rage. "Do not think this is something I will forget. Ahiga never forgets. One day your family will know what it is to suffer." The man paused for a moment, staring intently at Richard. Richard growled, bearing his teeth, not breaking his gaze. The man slowly stooped down to scoop up the woman in his arms before backing away between the trees and disappearing into the darkness.

Richard remained stationary for some time, shaken by what had happened. Plagued by an unpleasant hollow feeling in his stomach, he eventually sat on the ground, trying to steady his nerves. 'I can't believe I killed someone', he thought, deeply regretting having delivered the final bite to the female cougar's throat. 'I should have just wounded her, it didn't have to be a kill.' Realistically he knew two cougars would have been difficult to defeat if he hadn't killed one, and he had no reason to suspect they were people. Unfortunately though, knowing it had been a necessary kill didn't make him feel any less upset. The guilt washed over him, and he struggled to keep control of himself. 'Shake it off', he thought. Deciding it would be better to abandon his hunt and to head home, he made his way to the bush where he'd left his pyjamas. He changed his shape from a large sandy coloured wolf, back to his regular human form. Hurriedly he pulled on his garments before making his way back through the moonlit forest towards his home town.

He entered the house quietly and tiptoed up the stairs, not wanting to disturb Laura. Everything was dark and quiet; sure enough he could make out a lump under the blankets, and he heard the steady beat of Laura's heart. He almost hoped she'd wake up of her own accord, so he could confide in her about what had happened, but he knew he mustn't. He wasn't ready to reveal to her that he was a werewolf. Instead, he headed for the bathroom once again, seeing his red mouth and chin in the mirror. He splashed cold water onto his face, scrubbing with soap at the blood on his skin, which trickled into the basin. The sight of it made him feel like vomiting, as he remembered the fixed dead eyes of the female cougar before she changed back into a human. He wiped away the blood in the basin trying to rid it of the stains, as though it would somehow purge him of this feeling of guilt. It didn't work; he knew he couldn't take back what he had done. 'She's dead and it's my fault', he thought, squeezing his eyes shut for a second. 'It was self defence, but I didn't have to kill her.' His elbow jerked out to one side as he brought his hand up to his face, and he accidentally knocked a pot of coloured contact lenses, which tumbled to the floor. He wore them far more often than he ought to, in an attempt to hide his true eye colour. Bending down he picked them up and stared at the pot. "I don't know how she hasn't seen these things", he muttered under his breath, placing them back on the shelf. For all her qualities though, Laura wasn't particularly observant, but Richard was still sure she would notice his glowing orangey-red eyes if he stopped wearing the brown lenses. He almost wished she would, because if she asked him about it, he'd be forced to sit down and have the 'big talk' with her. There would be no more excuses.

"Rich?" a bleary voice called from the bedroom.

"Damn", cursed Richard quietly. He hadn't meant to wake her up; it must have been from the clatter of the pot falling. "I'm… erm…just getting a drink", he whispered through the half open door. "Go back to sleep, it's not time to get up yet."

Laura mumbled something unintelligible. Richard waited for

a moment, holding his breath, hoping she would fall asleep again. He was rewarded by the sound of a quiet snore and he exhaled with relief. He was about to tiptoe back into the bedroom when a loud bleep sounded from his pager. It was still in his work shirt pocket where he had left it hanging on the bathroom hook. 'Shit!' he thought, praying it hadn't woken Laura back up again. He heard another snore. 'Thank God', he thought. He reached his hand into the fabric of his shirt and pulled out the device. He read the message.

'Come to reservation after work'

He knew at once who it was from. 'What the hell is Pat sending me messages in the middle of the night for?' he wondered, peering at the time on his watch which he had left on the bathroom counter. 'It's four in the morning!' Pat was Richard's best friend. They had met at university, but upon graduation Pat had returned to the Native American reservation where he had grown up. He'd wanted to become a doctor, but his parents had fallen ill and had persuaded him to return to take his place as the next leader of their people. They were quite traditional, unlike some other more modern reservations, and chose to live a fairly simple life. Pat hadn't told Richard very much about himself at first, but had opened up once realising his friend was a werewolf. Richard, too, had been glad to find someone he could confide in - he'd never experienced that before.

He furrowed his brow and re-read the message. 'It's not like Pat to be up so late', he thought. He turned his pager to vibrate mode in case Pat would send another message, but none appeared. He waited for a couple of minutes, then shook his head, put down his pager, and headed back to bed, hoping this time he would be able to clear his mind and get some sleep.

The next morning Richard awoke to the sound of the alarm. It was cruel to be getting up so early given the night he'd just had. He crawled out of bed, being careful not to disturb Laura, and headed down to the kitchen to make breakfast. Every day was the same routine; get up, make breakfast, brush teeth, put in contacts, get dressed and head out to work. This day was no different, and the job was even less interesting. The day at work had been a long and tiring one, and as the mid-morning sun shone in through the window, the clock seemed to be ticking painfully slowly. He looked up at it on the office wall, as he had at least a hundred times during the past hour, and sent a few evil thoughts in its direction. Despite his parents having advised him to take a more solitary occupation working from home, he had rebelled against their suggestions, and upon leaving university had taken a position at a small local supermarket, working in administration. He had his own office at the back of the shop, right next to a handy vending machine which dispensed cola in abundance.

"What happens if your temper flares when you're dealing with an aggressive customer, and you whip your claws out at them?" his mother had fretted.

Richard had only barely been able to dampen their fears by reassuring them he was nowhere near the customers. Even so, he wasn't sure they believed him. Usually he quite enjoyed his job. It was quiet enough that he didn't need to worry about anybody discovering his secret, but social enough that he didn't feel too much like a recluse.

Idly he rifled through today's stack of letters. The one on top was a letter from a cardboard box manufacturing company. He groaned. 'I don't feel like dealing with the manager of this place right now. The guy is a real jerk,' he thought, swivelling in his chair and holding the letter over his paper shredder, twitching slightly. It was tempting, but he knew he couldn't. He'd read it later though, he really couldn't be bothered at the moment.

"What else is there?" he muttered. "Junk, invoice, bank statement, another invoice…"

RING RING

The telephone made him jump. He'd been uncharacteristically twitchy since last night's nightmare, and the events that followed it. He grabbed the receiver, nearly dropping it in the process. "Good afternoon, Super Value Foods, how may I help you?" he yelped.

"Hi Richard!" a familiar voice chirruped down the line at him.

Richard relaxed. "Hi beautiful. What's up?"

"Well…" Laura hesitated, "don't be mad, okay?"

Immediately concerned, Richard sat up a little straighter in his chair. "What's the matter?"

Laura let out a short dry laugh. "Just listen, okay?"

Richard nodded, then realised she couldn't see him. "Er… yeah…alright."

"Well, it's about my parents."

Richard stiffened. His future in-laws were difficult at the best of times. "What about them?"

"They decided to give us an early wedding gift."

That wasn't at all what Richard had been expecting. "Oh?"

"They rang this morning before I left for work. They said they knew we've been stressed with all the wedding preparations lately, so they thought it would do us both good to unwind. They've booked us a break for this weekend."

It took Richard a couple of seconds to ingest this information. "What? Where?" he babbled, reeling slightly at Laura's parents' uncharacteristic impetuousness.

"It's at this treehouse place. Friday night until Sunday night. It looks nice. They have wooden chalet pods in the trees; there's a lake and cycling tracks and even horses. I know it's spur-of-the-moment, but they said we'd love it", said Laura. "They were really gushing about it."

"I…er…this is very sudden!" stammered Richard. "Friday as in tomorrow?"

"Yeah tomorrow. Apparently it cost them a fortune, and we're under strict instructions to enjoy ourselves", said Laura.

"I thought you said you were going out with some friends this weekend?" asked Richard, remembering something Laura had told him a few days ago.

Laura sighed. "I told them that, but they said they'd already booked it, so I guess we have no choice. Just pack some bags for us when you get home from work please, I'm working late tonight. Ooh sorry, I have to go, my boss is glaring at me. I'll see you later."

CLICK

Richard sat for a few minutes with the receiver still held to his ear. 'What are we going to stay in a forest near a lake for, when we live so close to a forest and a lake anyway?' he wondered. Then a sudden churning feeling hit his stomach. He slammed the phone back into its cradle and grabbed the lunar calendar from his desk in a panic. "Oh no! No, no, no!" There it was, as plain as day. "Tomorrow night's a full moon!" he groaned.

There had been so many wedding preparations to take care of recently that he hadn't been keeping track of the days properly. He had a rough idea that his lunar change was due, but he hadn't realised it was so soon. He'd assumed it was sometime next week. "I can't go on holiday this weekend, it's impossible", he moaned, rubbing his temples. 'Laura will be so cross though. Her parents will be really unimpressed, but it can't be helped', he thought. 'They'll just have to get over it. I'll tell Laura I've got to work all weekend.' He absent-mindedly chewed his thumbnail. 'I'll cook her a nice dinner tonight and let her down gently. Maybe the treehouse thing can be rearranged for next weekend instead.'

Something was niggling at him. "Oh no!" he groaned again, realising he was going to visit Pat after work. He bit his bottom lip. 'Well, Pat is going to have to wait', he realised. 'I don't have to live with him if he's grumpy, but Laura is another matter!' Shaking his head at having been put in such a predicament, he returned to the letter from the cardboard box manufacturing company. "Right Mr. Stick-Up-Your-Ass, let's see what you are going to gripe about today."

There were more than enough tasks to keep Richard occupied over the course of the remainder of the day. Merely dealing with the unpleasant curator of the box company had taken up a good two hours, and his boss had dumped a pile of invoices on his desk to check over, which was so high he struggled to see over it. Still, he couldn't concentrate; his thoughts insisted on meandering back to the strange dream and what had happened in the forest with the two shape-changing mountain lions. By the time his shift at work was over, he had made up his mind to try and seek out the man and beg his forgiveness. 'I didn't get to say sorry,' he thought, 'not that apologising will bring back the woman, but...I have to say sorry'. Guilt gnawing at his conscience, he rose from his chair and reached for his pale beige jacket from the back of his chair. It was brand new, and he liked the way the dark brown buttons stood out against the lighter material. 'Laura said she's working late today, so I've got enough time to have a look around the forest to see if I can follow the man's tracks from last night.'

"You finished checking those documents Ricky?" called a voice from the corridor.

Richard gritted his teeth. He hated when his boss called him Ricky. "Yes, all done", he replied, trying to sound cheerful.

"Good, good. I'd have kept you overtime if they weren't completed."

'Like hell you would', thought Richard with a grimace. He feigned a light-hearted chuckle and called goodbye, knowing it would do him no favours to say what he really thought. He left the supermarket and headed for his car, pulling out an old fishing rod from the trunk and hoisting it over his shoulder. Whenever he wanted to avoid any awkward questions about why he was wandering around in the woods, he carried fishing equipment with him. The supermarket wasn't far from the edge of the forest, so he left his car parked where it was, and set off on foot, strolling through the streets looking no different from any other person heading out for a spot of fishing. People actually passed through the town quite often from all over the country to make their way into the forest to fish, as this area was known for its plentiful whitefish, so for Richard it made for a good cover story. Nobody would suspect that a mild-mannered supermarket administrator with a penchant for fishing was actually a werewolf.

Reaching the path leading to the forest, Richard headed down it, and walked through the overgrown bushes and dense trees towards the place where he had been hunting the previous night. He remained alert, keeping an eye out for any sign of the man, but he couldn't see or smell anything untoward. As a werewolf, his senses were naturally amplified, and he knew he would have been able to tell if Ahiga, either in human or cougar form, were present. He reached the area where he had fought the cougars, and set down his rod. 'Cumbersome thing', he thought, glad to be temporarily rid of it. For a moment he weighed up his options. He could either change into a wolf, or remain as a man. 'If I'm a wolf, I'll be able to track better, and I'll be faster, but I will still not be able to apologise.' After dithering for a couple of minutes, he opted to remain as he was, and started walking in the direction he'd seen Ahiga leaving the night prior.

To begin with, it was easy enough to follow Ahiga's tracks. His footsteps had left heavier impressions on the ground due to the weight of carrying the woman, and the scent of both of them was strong. After some time though, the footsteps and scents became mingled with those of other people, and to Richard's surprise, he also picked up the trails of several different animals. "That's definitely a bear", he muttered, lifting his nose to sniff the air. "Then again, I'm seeing wolf paw-prints here, and…surely that's not the scent of an owl on this branch?" Completely baffled by this seemingly random array of animal trails, he cautiously proceeded onwards. 'Can these Yee Naaldlooshii people turn into any creature?' he wondered, remembering the mountain lion skins he had seen yesterday. 'How weird.' He jumped at the sound of a loud screech from somewhere high in the trees. He looked up, just in time to see an eagle soaring high above his head, a little below the forest canopy, ducking and weaving through the branches of the many trees.

Richard felt uneasy, as though he was being watched. He proceeded on a few more steps, but already the seeds of doubt were rendering him reluctant to continue. 'Maybe I should just leave it and turn back', he thought, worriedly. 'There could be a huge tribe of these Yee Naaldlooshii people, and I wouldn't stand a chance against more than three or four at the most if they decide to jump me.' He hesitated, then turned around, but as he did so his toe caught on something and he stumbled. Immediately he felt a crunch beneath his feet. It made a loud noise, startling him. He looked down and gasped at the sight of a smashed human skull, almost hidden underneath the bracken. "Oh my God", he whispered, bending down and pushing aside the bracken ahead of the skull. Bones littered the area; some were half buried in the dirt, but others were haphazardly dumped on the ground, with bracken and leaves scattered over them. 'Someone has left these here intentionally', he realised. The local newspapers had featured a small article about the town cemetery having suffered a spate of recent acts of grave robbery. 'Are these the remains of those bodies?' he wondered.

A shiver ran down his spine, and he knew for certainty he wasn't going to be making that apology after all. Without hesitation, he began to run back through the forest in the direction of the town, quite forgetting his fishing rod in the process.

Richard looked at the time on his watch. 'Damn, I don't have much time; I need to cook dinner for Laura before she gets home', he thought, jumping over branches and thorns, moving fast through the trees.

CHAPTER FOUR

Staring in dismay at the blackened chicken on the baking tray, Richard sagged his shoulders, feeling miserable. Laura would be home any minute, and his hope of softening the blow about being unable to go on the weekend break with her had now gone to cinders, much like the dinner. 'Maybe I could whip something else up quickly?' he thought in desperation, flinging open the cupboard doors and rummaging through the various tinned goods stored there. Dejectedly, he closed the door again. 'I don't think cream of tomato soup, or baked beans, classes as a fantastic dinner', he thought. 'I wish I hadn't wasted time by traipsing around the forest after work. I wouldn't have put the chicken on such a high heat.'

The sound of a key in the front door lock signalled Laura's arrival. She let herself in. "Hi, I'm home!" she called.

"I'm in here", said Richard, trying to muster up some enthusiasm.

"What's up?" asked Laura as she headed towards the kitchen. She'd evidently picked up on his sombre tone. "Are you okay?" She stopped in the doorway, surveying the scene before her. "Oh, you burnt dinner."

Richard exhaled loudly. "Yeah", he admitted. He took three steps over to the trash can and threw the unfortunate remnants of poultry into it. "I was going to cook you a fancy dinner, but my culinary skills are less than spectacular."

"That's not like you. I don't think you've ever burnt a single dish in the two years we've been together", pointed out Laura. She narrowed her eyes. "Are you feeling alright?"

"Yes, I'm fine."

"Are you sure?"

Richard was just about to reassure her that he was quite well, but he stopped himself as an idea popped into his head. "Well, to be honest, no I'm not very well. I think I'm coming down with something", he lied. "I'm feeling sick, and my head hurts. I'm dizzy..." he paused, "and my legs are aching".

"Oh wow, that's not good", gasped Laura. She hurried towards him and pressed her hand against his forehead. "Hmm you don't feel warm. I don't think you have a temperature. Maybe you should just go and lie down."

Richard nodded emphatically, then realised he probably ought to put on a better display of invalidity. "Ohhhh owwwww my head", he groaned, lifting his hand to his forehead. "I'm sorry beautiful, but if I'm like this tomorrow, we're going to have to postpone our weekend break."

Laura's face fell, and Richard immediately felt guilty. "I hope not", she said with an anxious tone. "My parents said was non refundable, and those treehouse pods are now fully booked for the rest of the year. Mom told me it was just lucky when they made their enquiries about them because there had been a cancellation. You know what my parents are like...I'd rather not disappoint them."

'I hate it when she looks at me with that sad expression', thought Richard. The funny thing was that his stomach really *had* started to hurt. 'That'll be the stress", he thought. "I'm going to go and lie down", he said. "Can you fix yourself something to eat?"

"There's some fish in the freezer. Don't worry about me. Do you want anything?" asked Laura.

"No thanks", replied Richard.

"Okay, well you go and rest." She gave him a little shove towards the stairs.

Richard trudged up to the bedroom, an uncomfortable feeling of being at fault inside him. 'Better for her parents to lose the money though than to risk harming or killing someone by going on a vacation during the full moon', he thought. He reached the bedroom door, went inside, and eased himself onto the bed, letting out a groan which he knew would be audible from downstairs.

"Do you need anything?" called up Laura.

Richard felt another pang as he knew she was truly taken in by deception. "No thank you, I'll be fine", he replied weakly.

Laura didn't respond further, and Richard sank back against the pillows. 'It's for the best', he thought.

KNOCK KNOCK KNOCK

Richard sat up straight with a start and glanced in surprise at his watch. 'Who on earth could that be?' he wondered, listening to the urgent pounding on the front door.

Footsteps crossed the hallway, and he heard the click of a key turning. The voices drifted upstairs to his bedroom.

"Pat!" exclaimed Laura. "How lovely to see you. What an unexpected visit."

"Hello Laura", greeted Pat. Richard could hear from his tone that something was amiss. There was a nervous edge to his voice - subtle but definitely present.

"Won't you come in?" asked Laura cheerfully, seemingly not picking up on Pat's anxiety the way Richard had. "Richard is upstairs feeling sick I'm afraid, but you're welcome to stay for a drink."

"I...no thank you...I really must speak with Richard", stammered Pat. "I asked him to come to the reservation this evening, but..." he tailed off.

'Damn', thought Richard. He had completely forgotten about that message on his pager.

"Oh, really? He never mentioned it", said Laura. There was a brief pause. "If you like, you can go up and see him, but he might be asleep."

"Thank you", said Pat. Richard heard his heavy footsteps on the stairs as he ascended to the landing.

"Come in Pat", he croaked feebly, knowing Laura would be listening.

In the doorway stood a Native American man, in his mid-twenties. His long dark hair hung loosely around his shoulders, flopping over the collar of his blue chequered shirt. His dark brown eyes were filled with concern. "Richard, I must speak with you. I have been told you are ill."

Richard sighed, shook his head, and motioned for Pat to close the door. He knew he could be honest with his friend about why he had feigned being unwell.

Pat obliged and closed the door. He sat down on the edge of the bed. "What is the matter?" he asked.

"Laura's folks have booked a vacation for us this weekend", whispered Richard.

A look of understanding spread across Pat's face. "It will be a full moon", he said. "Now I see why you are hiding in the bedroom."

Richard nodded glumly. "I don't know what else to do. I can't tell her."

Pat raised an eyebrow. "Honesty is important between couples", he said sounding stern.

Richard clicked his tongue. "Let's change the subject", he suggested. "Is everything alright with you? I get the impression there's something on your mind. I'm sorry I couldn't come to the reservation, I was just…"

"You were busy pretending to be ill", supplied Pat. "Yes, I can see that, my friend. However you are right, I have a problem. I need your help. You must come with me now."

Richard glanced up at Pat. "But what about Laura? She'll realise I'm not ill!"

Pat frowned. "As your best friend, I am asking for your assistance on this urgent matter. Please do this for me."

Richard winced. Pat was as close to him as a brother, and he would have felt awful letting him down. He exhaled resignedly. "Okay, okay", he muttered, swinging his legs out of the bed. "This had better be serious."

They crept downstairs. Richard could hear his fiancée in the kitchen listening to the radio and singing along, painfully out of tune. "We built this city on rock and roll!" she screeched.

Richard chuckled. The song had only been released two weeks ago, but already Laura had claimed it as her new favourite record. She was obviously not aware that the two men were no longer in the bedroom. 'With a bit of luck she may just assume we're still upstairs talking', he thought hopefully. He and Pat headed to the front door wordlessly, opened it, and left the house.

"Okay, are you going to tell me what was so urgent that you felt the need to drag me out of my sick bed?" asked Richard, once they were some distance down the road.

"You were not really sick", pointed out Pat. "There is not a minute to lose. We have to rescue a little girl."

Richard raised an eyebrow. "Can't the fire department do that? They're good at rescuing people."

"Do not be absurd. She is not stuck up a tree like a stranded cat", retorted Pat sounding cross.

"So explain then", said Richard. "Is she from the reservation?"

"No, she is a shadowdancer."

Richard blinked. "A what?"

Pat let out a groan of exasperation. "I do not have time to get into this. We cannot just stand here. We have to get to the reservation quickly! Can you carry me?"

Richard didn't flinch at the strange request. He knew what Pat meant. They would travel much faster if he were in wolf form with Pat on his back. "I suppose so", he grumbled, still feeling irritated by Pat's vagueness. "Wait until we reach the forest."

They walked briskly together to the edge of the town. A huge thick expanse of trees lay to one side, stretching out for hundreds of miles. Once they had slipped through a gap in the chicken-wire mesh fencing which had been erected to keep wild animals from wandering into the populated area, Richard headed behind a tree. He preferred to change into a wolf in private.

"Pick up my clothes once I've changed", he called to Pat. Then he quickly pulled off his garments and deposited them in a pile on the floor, until he was standing naked. A chilly breeze whipped at his skin and he gave a little shiver. He tossed his clothes towards his friend, then closed his eyes and concentrated for a brief moment. He felt the familiar ripple of pleasure course through his body as he changed from man to wolf, as he had done so many times before. It was always the same; a sensuous euphoric feeling which caused him to tingle.

"Come on, we must hurry", urged Pat. Richard emerged from behind the tree, his paws padding softly on the bracken littering the forest floor. Pat looked up expectantly. "Good, you will be able to get us there much faster now", he said with approval.

Richard stood still and allowed his friend to mount his back. Once Pat was seated comfortably, with a bag containing Richard's clothes slung over his shoulder, the wolf began walking briskly in the direction of the reservation. He winced a little when Pat pulled his fur, but didn't falter in his speed. 'Is he going to bother telling me what the deal is with this kid then?' he thought, feeling irritable. He was worried Laura would realise he had gone out, and that would make it even more difficult to convincingly wriggle out of the vacation her parents had booked. He whined to catch Pat's attention.

"What is the matter?" asked Pat in surprise, wobbling dangerously astride the wolf. Richard couldn't answer, so he whined again. "Oh, the girl," began Pat, "she is trapped in the land of the dead". He paused to duck under a low branch, then began to speak again. "Her family are witches…shadowdancers. The child was experimenting with spells far beyond her understanding. She has disappeared, and her parents believe she has accidentally caught the attention of Bakwas, the King of Ghosts. According to legend, he lures people to the land of the dead, and is known for kidnapping children. There have been whispers among my people, claiming they have seen him. It is strange, as there has been no mention of him for a long time. My people believed he had been banished."

The mention of the name Bakwas jolted Richard, and he stopped walking, his heart thumping. The memory of the nightmare he'd had about being kidnapped as a child came flooding back to him again. 'It couldn't have been real', he thought in alarm. 'There's no way…surely it was just a dream? I didn't think there was *really* somebody called Bakwas.' He whined a little, trying to indicate to Pat that he wanted to know more.

"The shadowdancers came to us seeking our help. We were their last resort. They have exhausted every spell they can think of, but what they require is someone who can spirit walk", continued Pat. "This is why I need your assistance."

'Oh hell, what if it *was* real? Oh God no!' Richard felt as though he could barely breathe. 'Was I really kidnapped by that monster when I was a kid? The girl...oh God, the girl I accidentally banished...' He gulped, remembering how he had failed to save her, and the gruesome memory of his friend Thomas being eaten alive. 'I can't go back there', he thought in terror. The idea of returning to that awful cabin was making him sweat. But maybe...oh hell...I suppose I'm the only possible candidate then, as I'm a werewolf', he thought, his heart sinking at the thought of what he was being asked to do. He wasn't aware of anyone else with the natural ability to spirit walk to the land of the dead; as far as he knew, this was a feature of being a werewolf. It was both a blessing and a hindrance, as travelling to the land of the dead was not always smooth sailing.

'I am sorry, I realise it is a lot to ask, but the girl is only six and her parents are desperate."

Richard swallowed hard and continued to walk, pondering over Pat's words. 'It had to be a kid, didn't it? He knows I'm not going to say no to helping a kid', his inner voice pointed out. 'I can't fail yet another little girl.' He let out a small growl and shook his head, trying to shake his fears. With Pat no longer speaking, they fell into silence as Richard hurried through the forest, dodging trees and deftly picking his way around bramble bushes and rocks, until at last the reservation was in sight. As Richard approached it, he slowed to a stop and allowed Pat to slide down from his back. Then he waited, but when the Native American didn't make a move to give him back his clothes, Richard stepped forward and nosed the bag.

"Oh, I am sorry", said Pat. "I was distracted." He handed the bag to the wolf, who carried it in his mouth behind a bush. There, with a ripple effect running the length of his body, and a loud sigh, Richard changed back into his human form once again and hastily pulled on his clothes. "Are you ready?" called Pat.

"I'm coming", said Richard, fastening his boot laces and striding towards Pat. He wasn't ready to tell his friend about his nightmare.

He still wasn't a hundred percent sure it was a real memory, or just a product of having heard about Bakwas somewhere else. "Where are the witches then?"

"They prefer to be called shadowdancers", explained Pat. "I left them with Olivia in the canteen."

Richard smiled as he watched his friend's face light up when he spoke of his wife. Pat and Olivia had been married from a young age, having been betrothed to each other for some time prior. Richard had never seen a couple more devoted to each other. He sighed, his thoughts flicking back to Laura. He loved her, but occasionally she seemed a little distracted. He put it down to tiredness from work commitments. Certainly her enthusiasm for this weekend break she had booked was refreshing. 'It's just a shame she picked the weekend of the full moon', he thought with a touch of sarcasm. "How's Olivia?" he asked.

"She is well," replied Pat, "but concerned about the missing child".

Richard nodded. 'I can imagine', he thought, remembering how Olivia always fussed around children like a mother hen. As they entered the reservation and walked through it, he noticed everything seemed quieter than usual. "Where is everyone?" he asked.

Pat sighed. "Most are with the girl's parents, but some are trying to find a way to bring her back from the land of the dead."

"With magic I presume?"

"Yes, but Bakwas is very powerful. Without you, I fear we would have no hope."

"Well, talk about putting the pressure on me", said Richard with a wry grin, trying to conceal his fear every time the name Bakwas was uttered.

"Sometimes I wish my father were still here to help", said Pat. "He was a wise chief. He would have known what to do."

"Don't sell yourself short", said Richard. "You're a great leader and your people respect you. Come on, let's rescue that kid."

They headed for the canteen at the far side of the reservation. It was a relatively new wooden building. Since becoming leader of the tribe, Pat had made a few changes to the area, such as construction and rearranging of huts. Richard thought his friend was handling his new responsibilities far better than he gave himself credit for. They approached the canteen and Pat reached out to push the door open. Richard could hear many voices chattering inside. Upon entering, he couldn't see the shadowdancers at all; they were obscured by the large crowd of Native Americans surrounding them. 'Looks as though nearly everyone from the reservation is in here', he thought, his eyes scanning the crowd.

"We are back. Let me through!" announced Pat in a loud authoritative voice. Almost immediately the chatter died down and people moved aside to create an aisle through the throng. A couple, approximately in their late thirties as far as Richard could tell, their eyes red as though they'd been crying, looked up at Pat and Richard as they approached. They were sitting on one of the long wooden benches pushed up against one of the canteen tables.

"Is this the werewolf?" asked the man standing up hurriedly. He wore a crumpled navy blue suit with a crooked tie. He looked like a businessman, ready to take off his clothes at the end of a hard day at the office. His short brown hair stuck out at all angles.

The woman, too, stood up; slower than her husband though. Her knee-length red and purple patterned skirt clung to her legs, and her blue blouse was buttoned up wrongly, as though she had flung it on in a hurry; the shoulder pads seemed somehow lopsided. Her hair was pinned up in a messy bouffant. She held onto the arm of a chair as if fearing she may faint. "Did you explain the situation?" she asked, looking at Pat in earnest.

"Yes, he will help. Richard is a good man, you have nothing to fear from werewolves."

Richard shuffled uncomfortably. He wasn't used to being discussed so publicly like this. He cleared his throat, feeling awkward. "Erm...hi...I'm Richard. Happy to help", he began nervously, holding his hand out in the general direction of the couple, not sure which of them he should address first.

The man hesitated for a fraction of a second before grabbing Richard's hand and squeezing it with a firm grip. "Richard," he said warmly, "I can't tell you how much we appreciate this".

The woman stepped forwards and placed her hand gingerly on Richard's arm. Her fingers were as cold as ice. "Please...bring back our daughter."

Richard smiled wanly and extracted his hand from the man's grasp. "I'll do my best", he said, trying to sound reassuring.

Pat turned to the score of curious faces surrounding them. "Go about your business, there is no need to linger here." With a wave of his hand he dismissed everyone, and the canteen cleared of people. All that remained was Richard, Pat, Olivia, and the worried couple.

"Mr. and Mrs. Walker, we only know what little you have told us, but perhaps you can fill us in on exactly what happened", said Olivia, smoothing her ruffled red skirt down and fiddling with the collar of her white blouse. Richard thought the simpler clothes worn by the people of this particular reservation were far more sensible than the enormous shoulder pads and neon leggings he saw in the high street stores so often. Olivia was naturally pretty, and never seemed to bother with makeup; she didn't need to.

The woman shook her head, a few stray strands of brown hair escaping from her bouffant. "We didn't know where she'd gone at first", she said, wringing her hands. "She had been playing all day, or so we thought. Wrenwood House, our home, it's quite large. It's not unusual for Fay and her sister to disappear for hours when they're exploring. They're very close in age; Tina is only ten months younger than Fay, so they're both six. They're always together. There are more than enough secret passages in that old house to keep them busy. It was only when the bell rang to call the girls to supper and they didn't come, that we realised they were missing. We searched the whole house and eventually found Tina sobbing in the library." Mrs. Walker broke off as tears poured down her face.

"She told us Fay had found a book of spells in the library she wanted to try out. It's an old notebook of some kind. To be honest we don't know that much about it. One of our shadowdancers found it many years ago in the forest. Fay has always been advanced for her age, early to read and master basic spells. I believe she thought she would impress us if she learned some new incantations", continued Mr. Walker looking solemn. "She apparently tried to persuade Tina to go with her into the woods, but Tina was afraid and didn't want to leave."

"That's why Tina was crying", wept Mrs. Walker looking utterly distressed. "She had waited for hours for her sister to return, but Fay never came back!" Mrs. Walker reached into her pocket and pulled out a tatty weathered book which looked oddly familiar. "This is the book she used, we found it where she had gone to practice."

At closer inspection of the book, Richard felt a jolt of memory. 'The notebook containing the banishing spell, the one which belonged to the girl's mother, this is one and the same', he thought. He felt his face draining of colour, turning from warm to freezing cold. "I suppose Tina had been too scared and confused to go and tell you both", he muttered, trying to sound casual. "Poor kid. So how do you know that Bakwas took Fay to the land of the dead?" He wanted to add 'especially as I might have banished him myself', but he kept that information to himself.

"We searched the forest but couldn't find her", said Mr. Walker. "Eventually we tried to perform a location spell, but it proved futile, which we couldn't understand."

"At that point we carried out another spell to see what had happened, and witnessed a dark figure approaching Fay. Then they both disappeared", said Mrs. Walker. She dabbed at her eyes with the back of her hand. "We had no idea what we were dealing with. It took several hours of research to discover the figure was the King of Ghosts, Bakwas. We tried…" the poor woman choked on her words, and clasped her hand to her mouth, trying to compose herself. "We tried to summon him, to beg him to return our little girl, but nothing seemed to work."

"We have other shadowdancers living at Wrenwood House, but despite our best attempts Bakwas seemed unreachable", said Mr. Walker. He furrowed his brow. "We had nowhere else to turn. We knew there was a reservation not too far away, and we hoped someone here would know more about Bakwas than we did."

Pat rubbed his chin and frowned. "It would take dark magic to reach the land of the dead, or…"

"Or a werewolf", supplied Richard, realising what he was getting at.

"Yes", Pat agreed. He grinned. "I suppose you have to be useful for *something.*"

"Very funny", said Richard, not being serious himself. He looked back at the Walkers who were staring at him with anguished expressions on their faces. He dropped his smile and stood up a little straighter. "Rest assured Mr. and Mrs. Walker, I'll do my best to bring Fay back to you", he said, trying to sound confident.

"Bakwas will not release the child voluntarily", stated Pat. His normally cheerful face contorted with a frown.

'You can say that again', thought Richard. He remembered all too well what he was dealing with. Still unsure whether his nightmare had been a vision or in fact a memory, at this point it hardly seemed to matter. It was enough for him to know that this would be no simple mission.

"Then we will fight that evil spirit", fumed Mr. Walker. "What gives him the right to start kidnapping children? It's horrific!"

Pat shrugged. "It is just…what he does. He brings the living across to the land of the dead."

"There is still hope of saving Fay though if she has not eaten any food offered to her by Bakwas", piped up Olivia. "Legends state that Bakwas' victims cannot leave the land of the dead if they eat his food, but if she has not…we may be able to rescue her."

Mr. Walker raised an eyebrow. "Isn't that a bit like the ancient Greek story of Hades and Persephone? Surely it is just a made-up tale?"

Pat shot him a look of incredulity. "You are a shadowdancer, in the company of a werewolf, yet you doubt your legends?"

Mr. Walker slumped his shoulders. "I guess you make a good point", he conceded.

"Besides, how do you explain the ancient Greeks having such a similar legend to algonquian tribes, if it were only a story?" asked

Olivia quietly. "Different names of course, but language variations cannot hide the facts behind the stories."

"There are many truths in this world", agreed Pat.

Richard had been listening intently to this exchange. "I studied Classical Mythology at college", he murmured, suddenly realising why he had always felt drawn to that particular field of study. "Who would have thought it was all true?"

Pat shrugged again. "Well this particular tale does seem to relate to Bakwas."

Richard nodded, still deep in thought. 'After the mention of Bakwas, seeing that book, and the suppressed childhood memory coming back last night, I can't deny the evidence. It really did happen to me.'

"We're wasting time talking about it though", interrupted Mrs. Walker. "Please…there's not a minute to lose."

"Let us make our way to a more comfortable place", suggested Pat, gesturing to the hard wooden chairs within the canteen. "My living room will be better."

CHAPTER FIVE

Richard followed Pat, Olivia, and the Walkers out of the building. They headed straight towards a wooden house with a green door next to the canteen. It was Pat's home; Richard had visited him there many times before. The living room was sparsely furnished with beanbags, and very little else. Olivia always grumbled to Richard that she wanted proper sofas and cupboards, but so far she hadn't managed to persuade Pat to buy any.

"Do we just…sit on these things on the floor?" asked Mr. Walker, screwing up his nose at the sight of the beanbags.

Pat frowned. "Yes, that is correct", he replied.

"I'm sorry, excuse my husband. Of course we sit on them", said Mrs. Walker hastily. She deposited herself on a large fat blue beanbag, shuffled awkwardly, and then tucked her legs up beside her. Everyone else followed suit, until all five people were seated on beanbags in a circle.

"So now what?" asked Mr. Walker, looking expectantly at Richard. "Do you have to meditate or something?"

Richard felt his neck growing uncomfortably warm at the realisation of how much these people were depending on him. His mouth felt dry and his palms were clammy. "I…erm," he gulped, "Yeah something like that."

"How many times have you visited the land of the dead before?" asked Mrs. Walker.

"Um…twice", mumbled Richard, realising his encounter with Bakwas and Dzunukwa actually meant it was three times, but not wanting to admit that. "The first time was an accident though."

"But you have done it deliberately?" pressed Mrs. Walker. "It worked, didn't it?"

Richard swallowed hard. "Yes, it did. It worked fine…" he said with hesitation, "but…"

"But what?" Mr. Walker gave him a stern stare.

"I may or may not have been stoned at the time." Richard looked down, not wanting to meet Mr. Walker's gaze.

"It was in university", explained Pat.

Richard dared to glance up, and saw the Walkers looking at him, both wearing expressions of dismay.

"Please tell me you don't need…that…to be able to do it again", begged Mrs. Walker.

"Oh no, no, no no", stammered Richard. "I'll manage just fine." He wondered if he was actually telling the truth. 'Shit, what if I'm unable to get to the land of the dead?' he worried.

"Of course he will manage very well", agreed Pat.

Richard flashed his friend a smile, and took a deep breath. "Okay, here we go." He closed his eyes and tried to concentrate. Allowing his mind to go blank, he began to visualise himself in the shadowy realm of the Shroud, the layer of the land of the dead closest to the real world plane. He felt his body growing lighter, and the air seemed somehow sweeter. 'I've done it!' he thought in delight. He opened his eyes, fully expecting to be surrounded by the foggy confusion of shadows and shapes he associated with the Shroud. To his utter disappointment though, he realised his jubilation was somewhat premature.

"I can't see him!" gasped Mrs. Walker, clutching her husband's arm. "Is he in the land of the dead?" To Richard she appeared to be slightly out of focus.

Pat inclined his head. "I would think so", he replied.

'No, damnit, I'm not', thought Richard with frustration. 'I've only phased out.' Phasing out was easy for him. It involved vibrating the body's molecules to another frequency, like changing a radio station. It meant he was now on a different plane to the other people in the room, so as far as they were concerned he was invisible. 'I'm not surprised they assume I've made it to the land of the dead,' he thought, 'but I haven't. Hell, I might not make it at all!' Determined not to let everyone down, He closed his eyes again and tried to channel his deepest emotions. He thought about anything and everything that might stir up within him grief, love, fear, or desire. Eventually he began to hear something that made his skin crawl.

The whispers were almost imperceptible to begin with, but gradually grew louder. He opened his eyes and was greeted with the sight of shadows all around him. Pat, Olivia and the Walkers were no longer visible. He shivered. He didn't like the Shroud; it was creepy and made him feel uneasy. The whispers filled his head and he wondered if this was how it felt to go mad.

"Please, someone help me", he implored, hoping one of the spirits might manifest into a form easier to communicate with. "I'm trying to find a little girl. She has been brought here by Bakwas."

The whispers grew louder and more intense. He jumped as something icy cold ran across the back of his neck. "We don't speak that name here", came a voice close to his left ear.

Richard leapt to his feet in a fright. He had the sensation of floating in the mist. A figure started to materialise before his eyes. "Grandfather?" he gasped in astonishment, as the imposing sight of a man in his early thirties stood before him. Richard had been only a boy the last time he'd seen his elderly grandfather. Now here he was, looking young and strong. Richard had browsed through countless family photo albums over the years, and he recognised the spirit in front of him from a photograph of his grandparents' wedding.

"Little Richard", smiled the spirit. "I've missed you."

The long forgotten nickname awakened a memory in Richard he had forgotten he'd lost. He remembered sitting on his grandfather's knee, eating toffees and listening to soul music. "I've missed you too, grandfather", he said. He felt, to his surprise, tears trickling down his cheeks. 'I haven't cried in years', he realised.

The wispy form of Richard's grandfather smiled at him. "What are you doing here, boy? I was in the upper world, but I sensed your distress."

"I...I'm not sure", replied Richard, searching the deepest corners of his mind in an attempt to remember. "I was looking for something..." 'Come on, think, this place is messing with your head!' He ran his fingers through his hair, desperately trying to get a grip over his own memories.

"Little Richard, you must not let the land of the dead ensnare you", warned his grandfather. "Take charge, my boy. What were you looking for?"

"Fairies?" mumbled Richard, feeling confused. "Why am I thinking of fairies?"

His grandfather shook his head. "There are no little people in this place."

"Fairies, Fairies…" muttered Richard. "Little people…fair folk… fey…Fay!" he exclaimed. Everything came flooding back all at once. "I'm trying to find a little girl named Fay."

"Is she dead?"

"No, she was brought here by Bakwas."

Richard's grandfather gasped and moved backwards. For a moment he faded before Richard's eyes, but then reformed. "We avoid him at all costs", he said, his eyes wide. "That evil creature calls himself King of Ghosts. King of kidnappers is more accurate."

"I have to bring Fay back; her parents are frantic", said Richard. The whispers still floating around his head were making it difficult for him to concentrate. It seemed every time the name Bakwas was mentioned, they grew more agitated.

"That monster doesn't take the children he captures to the Happy Hunting Ground", said Richard's grandfather. "He takes them to his wife Dzunukwa. They live in a house…" he paused and screwed up his face. "It's in the spirit realm, but it's almost a separate dimension altogether. He is the supposed King of Ghosts after all, so his home is his castle, so to speak."

"An actual castle?" asked Richard, confused. He didn't remember a castle in his dream, or his memory, if indeed it was a memory.

"No, a house in the woods. It's part of the land of the dead, but it's hard to reach. You have to be standing in the right spot."

Richard puzzled over his grandfather's words. "So if I return to the real world plane, stand in the right place where the house is located, and then concentrate to enter the land of the dead again, the house will appear?"

His grandfather nodded. "Yes, little Richard. Be warned though, it is dangerous. The King of Ghosts is bad enough, but in many ways Dzunukwa is even worse. You may have to become a wolf to fight her."

"I know they're dangerous", agreed Richard. "I know all too well." Then he realised what his grandfather had said. "Become a…" he broke off, his stomach flipping over at what he had been told. "I've always heard it's risky to change forms whilst spirit walking."

"Yes, it is", his grandfather simply replied."You may have no choice though."

Richard squeezed his eyes shut, suddenly overcome with a shooting pain in his temples. 'Turn into a wolf while in the land of the dead? It's unheard of!' he thought in a panic. After a few moments he realised the whispers had died away, so he opened his eyes.

The room looked the same as it had done before he entered the Shroud. "Grandfather?" he called softly, but there was no response. He inwardly kicked himself for not having even said goodbye. Then a new thought occurred to him. 'Where is everyone?' The house was quiet and still. Although he appeared to be in Pat's living room, he was alone. It was dark outside. 'I wonder if the Walkers have returned to Wrenwood House', he thought, standing up and striding across the room to peer out of the window. 'Oh hell, Laura will definitely be wondering where I am.' A sudden noise from behind made him jump.

"Oh, you're back!" exclaimed Olivia's voice.

Richard blinked rapidly as Olivia switched on the lights. "Yes, only just a few minutes ago", he confirmed, squinting.

"We waited for a long time but after a while we were falling asleep, so we went to bed", said Pat, stepping out from behind his wife.

"Where are the girl's parents?" asked Richard. "Have they gone home?"

"No. They are in the dormitory", replied Pat.

Richard knew where his friend was referring to, as he had slept in the large shared dormitory himself many times when visiting the Native Americans. Usually it was occupied by guests, or by youths of the reservation who had not yet built their own house but were finding it difficult to remain with their parents. If couples were having marital problems, sometimes one or the other would sleep in the dorm for a few nights while they worked out their differences. If people were renovating their house, often they used the dorm as temporary accommodation. It was a one-size fits-all building, with rows of beds lined up, and a shared bathroom. He snorted. "I wouldn't have thought Mr. Walker would be happy sleeping there", he said.

Pat smiled sadly. "He is forced to put aside many things for the sake of retrieving his daughter."

"Did you find her?" asked Olivia. "What happened?"

Richard wrinkled his nose. "No, I didn't, but I met my grandfather."

"Your grandfather?" exclaimed Pat. "Richard, you should not be disturbing the spirits."

Richard let out a small growl and put his hands on his hips. "I'm doing my best. Do you want my help or not?"

Pat stepped forwards and lightly touched Richard's arm. "I am sorry", he said with sincerity. "You are right, I should not have reacted so quickly."

Richard shrugged. "It's okay. Let's go and wake the Walkers so I can tell you all together."

"We'll change our clothes. Stay there", said Olivia, looking down at her nightdress.

Richard nodded. He sat on a beanbag and waited as Pat and Olivia disappeared down the corridor into their bedroom. Idly, he looked down at his hand and drew out his wolf claws from his fingertips, his nails changing size and form. He held them up and examined them closely - the way they curved, their smoothness, the sharpness of the points. 'I really hope I don't have to fight Bakwas and his wife in wolf form', he thought, feeling a shudder running along his spine. 'I don't want to encounter them again in any form', he thought.

"Do not tear my beanbags", said Pat, laughing as he appeared in the doorway.

Richard looked down in surprise. "I wasn't planning on it", he said, retracting his claws. "Is Olivia ready?"

"Almost."

"What time is it?"

Pat pulled a watch from his pocket. "It is just past four."

"Four in the morning? Oh God, Laura is going to kill me! Not to mention the fact I have to be at work in less than five hours", gasped Richard in dismay.

"It's Friday today, you can always phone in sick. Nobody will know the difference as you don't work over the weekend", said Olivia entering the room.

"Not like you, Olivia, to advocate deception", pointed out Richard, feeling quite shocked.

"I know," agreed Olivia, "but we're trying to save a little girl. It's a bit more important than writing letters and filing paperwork."

"Come. We should go to the dormitory", said Pat.

Richard stood up and followed Pat and Olivia out of their house. He watched as they held each other's hands as naturally as breathing. Laura never wanted to hold his hand these days. She said public displays of affection were only for teenagers. Richard couldn't help being a little jealous of the closeness between Pat and Olivia, and wondered if he and Laura might re-strengthen their own bond after the wedding. 'The weekend break might have done a lot to shake off the dry spell we've been having lately,' he thought ruefully, 'if only her parents had booked it for *next* weekend'.

They reached the dormitory and quietly went in. It was dark, but Richard's keen werewolf eyes quickly adjusted to the surroundings and he began to make out shapes of beds. "Stay here, I'll find them", he whispered to his friends. He knew he wouldn't really need to rely on his vision anyway, as his highly perceptive sense of smell easily led him through the room, and down to the two beds where the Walkers were sleeping side by side. Without saying a word, he reached out and patted Mr. Walker, who was still fully dressed. He bolted upright with a start.

"Fay?" he shouted. His voice echoed through the dorm, and several sleeping Native Americans began to stir.

"Shhh!" hushed Richard urgently. "Stop shouting", he whispered. "It's me, Richard. Wake your wife, we need to talk."

Richard could hear Mr. Walker's heart racing, but the man nodded, and leant over to the next bed to tap Mrs. Walker's shoulder. "Wake up honey. The werewolf is back. We have to speak with him about Fay."

'I have a name you know', thought Richard indignantly, but he said nothing. Mrs. Walker mumbled and wriggled under her blankets.

"Come on Barbara, wake up", urged Mr. Walker.

The sleepy woman flung back her bed cover and staggered to her feet. Her dress was crumpled and her short brown hair dishevelled, but she held onto her husband's arm, shoved her feet into her shoes, and shuffled after Richard out of the room. Once outside the dormitory, Mr. Walker closed the door behind them, and they followed Pat back to his house.

"Your reservation is very...quaint", said Barbara blearily.

Pat raised an eyebrow. "Ummm...yes. Well, we need to hear what Richard has to say." Pat looked over at his friend, visibly relieved to be passing the discussion to someone else.

Richard cleared his throat. "I managed to learn some useful information while I was in the land of the dead", he began, looking anxiously at the expectant faces surrounding him. "Bakwas has taken Fay to his house in the woods."

Mr. Walker leapt to his feet. "We must go there!" he exclaimed. "Where is it?"

Richard sighed. "It isn't as simple as that", he explained. "It's in the land of the dead. We have to go to the place in the forest where the house is situated, and then access it by entering the Shroud."

"Okay..." said Barbara slowly. "So where is that?"

"That's the problem. I...I don't know", confessed Richard, hanging his head. "I was ejected from the Shroud before I could find out its exact location."

"Well, I suppose we could try a locator spell, but I don't know if it would be of any use", said Mr. Walker, sounding doubtful. "We tried to find Fay using magic, but it didn't work, something was blocking it. I cannot imagine a spell to locate this house would be any more successful."

Richard felt his heart sink. "Well, we need to find it, otherwise there's very little I can do", he pointed out.

"Once we find it," said Olivia, "then what?"

"If Fay hasn't eaten anything I might be able to bring her back with me, but I'm going to have to contend with both Bakwas and his wife Dzunukwa."

Olivia gasped and her hands flew to her face. "Oh no", she whispered.

Barbaras eyes widened. "What? What's the matter?"

"Oh...erm...nothing", stammered Olivia.

"Tell us, please", insisted Mr. Walker.

"It's nothing, really, only myths and stories that's all. Bakwas' wife is not known for her pleasant nature."

"You and Pat both pointed out that myths and stories hide many truths", said Mr. Walker pointedly. "What is it?"

Olivia bit her lip. "Dzunukwa is known for cannibalism", she mumbled. "And she's exceptionally large."

Barbara winced. "We have to rescue Fay immediately", she said. "Finding that house is our priority."

Pat looked pained. "There is one thing we could try..."

"Oh no, Pat, you mustn't even consider using dark magic", cried Olivia.

"Perhaps not me, but one of the shaman here at the reservation might do it."

"Pat, I'm surprised at you. It's not right to ask someone else to dabble in such dangerous arts", chided Olivia.

"We'll do it; we'll do it together; whatever is necessary", said Barbara. She turned to her husband. "Right?"

Mr. Walker nodded. "Yes, anything. We can't lose our daughter."

Richard bit his lip. He had been listening to this conversation without interjecting. He wanted to tell them all about his nightmare, and explain there was a possibility he'd been kidnapped by Bakwas and Dzunukwa himself as a boy, but now it seemed too late. 'They'll wonder why I waited so long to mention it', he thought.

KNOCK, KNOCK, KNOCK!

A rap at the front door made Richard jump. Pat frowned. "Who could be here at this time?" he said.

"Oh hell, I hope it's not Laura", groaned Richard.

"Who is Laura?" asked Barbara, as they watched Olivia cross the room to answer the door.

"She's my fian…" began Richard. Then he stopped and breathed a sigh of relief to see a teenage Native American standing in the doorway. The boy's hair was short and black, and he wore a pair of black trousers teamed with a plain white t-shirt. Pat looked over at the Walkers. "This is Kingfisher, Olivia's younger brother."

"Richard!" exclaimed Kingfisher. "What are you doing here?"

"Hi King", said Richard, smiling. He got on well with Kingfisher. The boy had recently turned eighteen, but instead of deciding to go to university as Pat had done, he'd opted to remain in the reservation and take on a more traditional role. Richard believed it was really because Kingfisher had his eye on a girl he lived close to and couldn't bring himself to leave her, but it was only a hunch.

"It's late King. Why are you awake?" asked Olivia, sounding motherly.

Kingfisher shrugged. "I was sleeping in the dorm. I had an argument with father yesterday so I thought it was better to make myself scarce. I heard voices and people walking around not long ago, so I thought I'd investigate."

"You were arguing with father? Again?" groaned Olivia rolling her eyes.

"He treats me like a child", protested Kingfisher. "You are only a few years older than me, yet he sees you as a woman since you married Pat. It's not fair."

"Stop pouting. He will realise soon you are all grown up, but you should prove it by not acting so defiantly", advised Olivia.

Kingfisher grunted. "Anyway, what's going on here?"

Olivia shot a sideways look at Pat and the Walkers. "Should I tell him?" she asked.

The Walkers gave a curt nod, and Pat signalled his approval. "This is Mr. and Mrs. Walker", said Olivia. "Their daughter has been taken by Bakwas. We're trying to help them bring her back."

Kingfisher's eyes widened. "Wow, that's dangerous! Is there anything I can do to help? I've been studying to be a shaman."

"No, I do not think so", said Pat. "Thank you, but you are right, it is dangerous. We will have to use powerful dark spells."

Kingfisher looked hesitantly at the Walkers. "Do they know about magic?"

Mr. Walker nodded. "Yes, sonny, we do. We're shadowdancers; witches."

Kingfisher looked impressed. "So, couldn't *your* magic bring back your daughter?"

Mr. Walker clicked his tongue in annoyance. "No."

"I'm sorry", said Kingfisher. "Don't worry, I'm sure we'll rescue her."

Barbara gave him a weak smile. "How are we going to find Bakwas' house?" she asked, turning to Pat.

"We will require a blood sacrifice", replied Pat, sounding grave. "Our magic is different to yours. We have to channel the spirits and appease the Great Spirit, Gitche Manitou. This spell will go against my teachings, but I see no other way to locate the house. I only hope I do not anger the spirits greatly."

"I can catch a rabbit or something for the blood sacrifice", said Richard, knowing he was by far the most efficient hunter of the group.

"I don't like this at all", said Olivia. "There must be another way?" she implored, looking at her husband. "We shouldn't meddle in sacrificial magic."

"How do you even know what we're supposed to do?" asked Richard, looking curiously at Pat.

"I have read many books", he replied. "I recall one book

detailing a way to locate objects hidden by the land of the dead. It was not a book I should have read, but I was curious. I never thought I would use the information from within its pages."

"I'm sorry", said Barbara, a tear falling down her face. "I did not mean to involve you in anything you're not comfortable with, but Fay means the world to us."

Pat placed his hand on her shoulder. "I know", he said gently. "Do not worry, we will find the house." He turned to Richard. "Please go now, and find an animal."

"Okay", said Richard, not fazed by the abrupt way his friend had asked. He was used to Pat's accent, and his sometimes unintentional brusqueness.

"I'll come with you", piped up Kingfisher. "I love watching you hunt."

Richard smiled. "Alright King." He looked back at Pat. "We won't be long."

CHAPTER SIX

Leaving the house, Richard and Kingfisher headed out of the reservation towards the forest. Richard automatically began walking in the direction of a nearby area he knew was usually teeming with rabbits. Kingfisher fell back. "What's the matter?" asked Richard, stopping to turn around.

"I can't see where I'm going", admitted Kingfisher sounding sheepish. "I forgot to bring a flashlight."

Richard rolled his eyes. "You're not going to be able to see me hunt", he pointed out.

"I know. I wanted to discuss something with you anyway though. I...could use some advice."

Richard walked back over to Kingfisher and offered the boy his arm. "Here, hold onto me. I'll guide you and we can talk as we walk. We can't waste any time stopping; Fay's life is at stake."

Kingfisher held onto him, and together they continued through the forest. "So..." began Kingfisher, hesitating, "can I ask you something?"

"Sure."

Kingfisher sighed. "How did you figure out what to do with your life?"

Richard snorted. "Who said I have anything figured out?"

"Well, you know what I mean. You went to university; how did you know you wanted to do that? Were your parents happy for you? What about Laura? She's not a werewolf, so how did you decide she was the right person for you?"

"That's a lot of questions", remarked Richard. He exhaled. "I always wanted to be an accountant, and I knew I'd need some further education. My parents weren't exactly thrilled about it because they thought I'd be leaving myself open to becoming discovered, but I followed my heart."

"But you're *not* an accountant", pointed out Kingfisher.

"Well, I sort out the company's finances, among other things", said Richard. "It's not ideal, but it pays the bills, and it's as close to what I wanted to do as I can manage."

"And Laura?"

"Oh I just knew she was the right one. You can't mistake that feeling. When you know, you know." He paused. "Are you having trouble deciding what to do with your life?"

Kingfisher nodded. "My parents don't want me to leave the reservation, but I want to be a lawyer. Then there's the fact I kinda wanted to ask Dyani on a date, but I'm scared."

"It's okay to be scared, but ask her anyway. Follow your heart and the rest will sort itself out." Richard felt as though he was regurgitating the inscription from a motivational poster, and he wasn't sure how much of it he believed himself, but it sounded like the right thing to say. To his relief, Kingfisher seemed happy enough with his answer.

"So whatever I feel is right, I should go for, even if it's against my parents' wishes?" Kingfisher asked sounding hopeful.

Richard nodded. "It's your life, not theirs." He stopped walking abruptly, realising where they were. "We're almost there, we have to stay quiet", he whispered. "Come on."

They tiptoed through the bushes, trying hard not to step too heavily on twigs and branches underfoot, for fear they would snap loudly. "It's too dark for me to see anything", whispered Kingfisher. "I'll wait here." He let go of Richard's arm and sat on the roots of a tall tree.

Richard silently made his way around to the other side of the tree and slipped off his clothes, passing them round to Kingfisher. "Hold these please", he whispered. Then, smoothly he transformed into a large sandy coloured wolf. The ripple which coursed through his body caused him to shudder with pleasure. When he had been a teenager, he'd once spent the best part of an entire day shifting back and forth from human to wolf; it was close to orgasmic. The next day though he'd come down with a blinding headache, and realised that perhaps changing shape ninety-something times in a row was not the greatest idea he'd ever had. He padded out from behind the tree and crept forwards a few feet, sticking his nose through a bush in order to sniff the clearing beyond. The smell was unmistakeable. 'Rabbits', he thought. He waited a few moments until the scent grew stronger. The creatures were moving closer to him. 'Silly things with no sense of perception', he thought, scoffing at how easily the rabbits overlooked his presence. 'Just a second more', he thought, then suddenly he leapt out of the bushes directly onto an unsuspecting rabbit. Usually it was quite straight forward - a quick bite and the animal was killed. This time though he had to make sure it remained alive, which made things trickier. He held down the squirming creature with one paw, whilst trying to gently take hold of the skin at the back of the rabbit's neck with his teeth in order to carry it. This proved to be more awkward than he could have anticipated. 'For God's sake, isn't this how real animals carry their young?' he thought, irritated by how uncooperative the rabbit was being. Finally, he managed to pick up the squeaking creature and carried it back to where Kingfisher was still waiting.

"Richard, is that you?" asked Kingfisher, sitting up straighter and trying to squint through the darkness. Richard let out a whine in response. "Oh good, did you get a rabbit?" continued Kingfisher.

'How does he expect me to answer him?' thought Richard. He walked over to the youth and bent down, allowing the rabbit to dangle over Kingfisher's lap.

"Oh!" exclaimed Kingfisher, taking hold of it. Richard kept a firm grip on the animal until he was sure his friend wasn't going to accidentally release it.

'I sure as hell don't feel like catching another one', thought Richard. He picked up his clothes with his teeth and hurried again around the back of the tree to return to human form and get dressed. "You still got that rabbit?" he called pulling on his trousers.

"Yes. Wriggly little thing", replied Kingfisher. "Seems a shame to kill it."

"I suppose it can't be helped", said Richard. "If it makes you feel any better, maybe we could eat it afterwards."

Kingfisher let out a hollow laugh. "You wouldn't want to eat something which has been used in a ritual. It wouldn't be safe."

Now dressed, Richard returned to Kingfisher. The forest wasn't quite as dark as it had been previously, and he realised dawn was beginning to break. He looked at Kingfisher, curious. "What kind of magic is it that Pat will be using?" he asked.

"We're not supposed to talk about the Ways", he replied. "Not in any detail anyway. I…I guess I can tell you a little though."

"The Ways?"

Kingfisher nodded. "There are many Ways in Navajo magic; that's what we call them. Some Ways are particularly associated with negativity. The Witchery Way, 'Áńt'įįzhį, is the worst. Practitioners carry out all sorts of terrible deeds. They murder their family members, they skin people, and sometimes they are involved in cannibalism, necrophilia, incest…" Kingfisher tailed off.

"Wow how awful", gasped Richard.

"It's not unheard of for hunters to mistake werewolves for áńt'įįhnii, those who live by the Witchery Way, because they wear the pelts of other creatures and can change shape."

"Oh you mean Yee Naaldlooshii", realised Richard, his mind immediately flooded with images of the bones in the forest, and the cougar shape-shifters. "I've…erm…heard of them."

Kingfisher shuffled uncomfortably. "In your tongue, Yee Naaldlooshii would be called skinwalkers, but we should change the subject", he said. "I've told you way too much already."

"Well, presumably Pat wouldn't be doing anything like that", said Richard, relieved Kingfisher hadn't asked how he knew of skinwalkers.

Kingfisher's eyes widened. "I should say not! No, no way. He will more than likely use a spell from the Frenzy Way I should imagine."

"What does that involve?"

"The Frenzy Way uses charms, and it more or less influences other people. It can affect their mental state. It could be used to show someone visions, so perhaps we might see the location of Bakwas' house."

"God, I hope he knows what he's doing", said Richard, concerned. "Mr. and Mrs. Walker were offering to perform the spell themselves."

Kingfisher wrinkled his nose. "I'm not sure that would be very successful. They may know magic, but it is very different to the Navajo Ways. Their magic might clash with it."

"Sounds complicated", said Richard. "Come on, let's get this rabbit back to the reservation before I eat it. I'm getting a little hungry. I burnt my dinner."

There didn't seem any need to talk as they made their way back. Kingfisher managed to walk without guidance thanks to the lightening sky, and Richard hurried on ahead, having re-taken possession of the squirming rabbit. 'I could really use a nap right now', he thought, blearily stumbling on a tree root. He pressed on, knowing how urgent it was that he return swiftly, and began to sprint, leaving the youth behind. Finally he reached the reservation and headed straight for Pat and Olivia's house.

Pat flung the door open before Richard even had the opportunity to knock. "Do you have it?" he asked.

Richard nodded and thrust the rabbit into Pat's arms. The creature squeaked in terror. "It isn't a very co-operative bunny", he said.

Pat stroked the creature's soft brown fur and whispered a few Navajo words into its ear. At once the rabbit stopped struggling and calmed down, its nose twitching. "I do not blame it for being afraid", he said. "This sacrifice is regrettable."

The sound of running feet and panting behind Richard caused him to swing around to see who was approaching. "Kingfisher! Come on, hurry up!" he called, as the boy puffed towards them.

"Shhh", hushed Pat. "People are sleeping."

Richard looked sheepish. "Sorry."

"Richard, you're so fast", complained Kingfisher, reaching the house.

"Maybe you're just out of shape", said Richard, grinning.

"I think we should go to the forest to carry out this spell", said Pat. "I do not want anyone else from the reservation to see us performing spells from 'azhįįtee; they would disapprove. Wait here; I will fetch the others." He closed the door, leaving Richard and Kingfisher outside.

"You have to be kidding me", moaned Kingfisher. "We just came from the forest and now we're going back again? I should have just stayed there."

Richard was only half-listening. "What's 'azhįįtee?" he asked, recalling what Pat had just said.

"What? Oh, that's the Frenzy Way I was telling you about. See, I told you that's what Pat would use."

Richard frowned. He was about to speak but at that moment the door opened and out trooped Pat, Olivia, and the Walkers. Barbara's face was pale and drawn, and she fiddled nervously with the rings on her fingers. "What if it's too late?" she fretted, turning to her husband. "What if she's already eaten the food Bakwas gave her?"

Mr. Walker put his arm around his wife. "You mustn't think like that", he said, his voice trembling. "She'll be fine."

"You can't possibly know that", said Barbara, a tear escaping her eye and streaking down her face, dragging along with it a black smudge of eyeliner which was already smeared under her eyes.

"Come on, let's get on with finding the house", said Olivia.

They made their way into the forest, walking far enough away from the reservation so they would not be seen by anyone who might feel like taking an early morning stroll, and stopped in an area where the trees were not quite as close together. 'Not exactly a clearing, but it'll have to do', thought Richard.

Pat pushed aside several twigs and stones from the ground, and sat on a patch of moss. It was mainly dry peat and small clumps of grass in this clearing, so Richard opted for a tuffet of grass. When everyone was seated, Pat passed a backpack to Olivia. "I need the knife", he said. "Please would you get it out?" Olivia obligingly retrieved a large hunting knife from inside the bag and handed it to her husband.

"Are you sure you don't want us to perform the spell?" asked Mr. Walker.

"I do not believe you could", stated Pat. "This is Navajo magic. If you tried and it went wrong, I dare not think what the consequences would be."

Mr. Walker nodded. "Very well", he conceded. "Thank you; it means a lot to us that you are willing to help."

"Let him get on with it!" exclaimed Barbara, flapping her hand at her husband.

Pat held up the rabbit by its ears. The spell to calm it down had obviously been only temporary, for the poor creature began thrashing around in a wild fit, its legs kicking out in all directions. Pat closed his eyes and started to chant in Navajo. Richard didn't understand what was being said. He picked up the word 'gah' meaning 'rabbit', and he heard Pat utter 'álííl' which he knew related to supernatural rituals, but the rest he couldn't translate. 'I never was very good with other languages', he thought, watching the rabbit's kicking foot swinging closer and closer to Pat's head. As Pat chanted, Richard could have sworn he saw lights flickering on and off, but when he turned to look at them, they disappeared. He began to feel light-headed and woozy. He thought he saw Olivia light a fire on the ground, but he couldn't be sure as everything was so weirdly confusing. Pat continued to chant, and Richard felt his head sway backwards and forwards uncontrollably, shaking from side to side at blurring speeds, his body began to shudder as he rocked to-and-fro. His eyes rolled back in his head, and Pat kept fading in and out of his vision. He saw Pat raise the knife and slit the rabbit's throat in one swift fluid motion. Then everything froze, like a snapshot of time. The whole scene became crystal clear, motionless, yet the fire still burned with flickering flames, and blood dripped from the frozen blade. He could not move, he could only observe as the drop of blood hit the ground, sending a ripple of white energy out from it.

As the energy passed through him, he immediately saw in his mind's eye a little girl, around six years old, sitting on a fallen log and surrounded by trees. A book was open on her knee, and the child appeared to be reading aloud from it, using her finger to trace across the words on the pages. Richard couldn't hear a sound, but the girl's lips were moving. Her hair started to blow across her face, and she lifted her hand to brush it away from her eyes. It seemed the wind in the area had picked up, for the trees were bending and swaying, their leaves flapping wildly. An eerie mist began to fill the clearing, and behind the child a pair of blood red eyes glowed from within the foliage, unnoticed by the girl, summoned by the very words she was uttering. Then through the haze a large shape began to form. At first, Richard couldn't make out what it was, but as the girl continued with her spell it became more visible. Richard realised it was a familiar looking wooden cabin.

His stomach lurched at the sight of it, yet he felt inexplicably drawn towards the building. He felt his body moving, but couldn't figure out what was happening. He didn't think he was moving voluntarily. He could see nothing now but the cabin; it was as though someone had glued a photograph of the building to the inside of his eyes. The picture was static, like a scene from a brief instance of time. Still he felt his body continue to move against his will, until at last he felt a sudden plummeting sensation in the pit of his stomach; the same sort of nerve-wracking feeling of falling one gets sometimes when just about to drop to sleep.

"Richard! Oh my God, Richard!" a voice called.

The screaming caught Richard's attention. 'Where is that noise coming from?' he thought absently. 'Sounds like someone is in distress.' The screaming continued. 'I wonder if someone died', he thought, hearing the voices ringing through his head. 'Who is Richard?'

"Please Richard, come back to us", begged a second desperate sounding voice.

'Hang on, *I'm* Richard', he realised. At that moment, five faces swam into his view. He gasped; he felt as though he had been pulled from quicksand. His throat was constricted and his tongue stuck to the roof of his mouth. "Water", he croaked. He felt someone push something to his lips and water began to fill his mouth. He drank the entire flask dry. "Ugh", he grunted. He looked around and saw he was lying on the ground, his head propped up on Olivia's knees. "I could drink that again", he panted.

"We thought you weren't going to make it", said Kingfisher, patting him on the shoulder.

"What happened?" asked Richard. "I saw Bakwas' house...at least I think I did."

"It was terrifying", whispered Barbara, her eyes wide. "Your eyes went black and you were babbling in some weird language none of us had ever heard before, and swaying. Then you started walking for ages through the forest like you were possessed!"

"You led us here", added Kingfisher. "Then you collapsed. We couldn't wake you!"

"Is this where the house is?" asked Mr. Walker. "Have you brought us here for a reason?"

Richard stared at Mr. Walker's hopeful expression. "I...I don't know", he admitted. "I did see a cabin. My body seemed to be out of my control. Didn't the Frenzy Way spell affect anyone else?"

"No", replied Olivia. "It's probably because you're a werewolf. Your ability to spirit walk made you the prime target of the spell."

"I believe the spell linked you to Fay, but there is only one way to find out if it worked", stated Pat. "You must enter the land of the dead again. I do not like it, but you must try."

Richard sat up and looked around; the sun was shining brightly. "Oh hell, I haven't told my boss I'm not going to be coming to work today."

"I will vouch for you, don't worry", said Mr. Walker. "I shall make it financially worth his while to turn a blind eye to your temporary absence."

Richard felt uncomfortable. "Um...it's okay...I'll just say I was sick." He looked around the clearing. "It's nice here", he said appreciatively. "We're not far from Wolf Lake. I go fishing there sometimes."

"You're stalling", pointed out Kingfisher.

Richard sighed. "I know. It's just...what the hell do I do once I've found Bakwas and his wife?" He knew what he ought to do, and that was not approach them in the first place, but for the sake of the little girl he knew he had to go through with it. 'Man up, Richard!' he told himself.

"Dzunukwa", supplied Olivia.

"Yeah...how am I meant to fight them?"

"You do not", said Pat looking serious. "You must try to enter unnoticed, and bring Fay back to the land of the living."

"My grandfather said I may *have to* fight them, and that I'd have to use my wolf form."

Pat's eyebrows shot up. "I certainly hope it will not come to a direct confrontation."

Richard nodded and took a deep breath. "Okay, here goes." He closed his eyes and tried to concentrate, but nothing happened. 'I'm not even phasing out', he thought in disgust.

"Why isn't it working?" whispered Barbara.

"I don't know, honey", said Mr. Walker looking concerned.

Richard looked at the couple sharply. "It would be really helpful if I could have some silence."

The Walkers looked a little taken aback, but they fell silent. Richard took a moment to compose himself, then tried again. However, despite summoning up as many emotional thoughts and memories he could think of, nothing happened. He shook his head sadly. "I can't, I'm sorry, it's not working", he said in a quiet voice.

"You must be exhausted", said Olivia; she sounded sympathetic. "Also, when is the last time you ate anything?"

"I...erm..." Richard screwed up his nose trying to think. "I had a couple of cookies at work yesterday lunchtime."

"It is no surprise you are struggling to enter the land of the dead", said Pat. "Your body needs sleep and food for energy."

"But time is of the essence", insisted Mr. Walker. "We must get Fay back before it's too late."

"You will not get her back at all if Richard cannot cross over to the Shroud", pointed out Pat. "He must rest."

Reluctantly, the Walkers made their way with Pat, Olivia, Kingfisher and Richard back to the reservation. Richard could tell they were unhappy about it, but he knew Pat was right; he wouldn't be of any use if he was unable to get to the land of the dead. "You have to promise not to let me sleep too long", he said, as they stopped outside Pat and Olivia's house. "Laura will wonder where I am if I don't return home this afternoon. She probably thinks I spent the night here and that I'm at work now, but if I don't go home later she'll come looking for me."

"Do not worry," said Pat, "I will wake you after three hours."

Richard nodded. "Okay, three hours should be fine. Then we'll head back here, I'll rescue the girl, and hurry home. I need to convince Laura I'm too ill to go on this trip this evening, which is not going to be easy given that she'll think I went to work today. Plus it's the full moon tonight so I need to persuade her to go out with her friends. If I'm not back in the forest by eleven-thirty, I'm going to have a serious problem."

Pat frowned. "I hope Laura does not ask many questions… unless you are ready to reveal your secret."

"Why would I do that?" sighed Richard, running his fingers through his hair. "I'd be dragging her into this crazy world of ours. There's no way, she'd freak out."

"Well, it is your decision", replied Pat, sounding dubious.

Richard flapped a hand at his friend. "Shush now, let's drop the subject. I'm going to get a nap. Don't forget to wake me." Then he turned around and made his way to the dormitory. It was quiet and empty; everyone was hustling and bustling around the reservation, busy with their lives. He selected the first seemingly unclaimed bed, flopped into it, and within seconds was fast asleep.

CHAPTER SEVEN

It didn't take long for an image to form in Richard's sleeping head. He was sitting inside a large cage, his knees huddled up to his chest, and he was wearing a red tattered dress. He forgot he was actually a man, for in his dream he had the mind of a child; a little girl. He could see through her eyes, and feel what she felt. He no longer thought of himself as Richard, but instead he believed he was this girl. Beside him was another girl, older, around twelve years of age, with long straggly blonde hair. It was matted and dirty and looked as though it hadn't seen a brush or comb for years. The cage they were sharing was inside a large wooden room, and everywhere there was an eerie mist which seeped in through cracks in the window and door frames.

"Maria...I'm scared", Richard said in a little girl's voice, weeping into his small hands.

The older girl put her arm around him. "I know, I know. There there."

Richard looked up at her and sniffled. "How long have you been here?"

"I don't know", Maria replied. "There isn't any way of measuring time in this place. I might have been here for only a little while, or perhaps a long time. I just...don't know. I'm their slave; I suppose I'll be here forever." She paused. "The cabin was here in the Shroud, but it was banished to the underworld for a while...I don't know how long. A boy was here and he cast a spell. I was supposed to be rescued, but something went wrong. I ended up being banished along with the cabin." One solitary tear escaped her eye and spilled down her cheek but she brushed it away crossly. "At least when we were in the Deep Void, those monsters couldn't capture any more children. Listen, don't ask me things like that, you're making me cry. I mustn't cry."

"Why not?" asked Richard, his own eyes welling up again.

Maria looked seriously at him. "They do terrible things to me if I cry."

Richard's bottom lip began to wobble. "Will they do terrible things to me if I cry too?" he asked.

"I…I don't think you want to know the answer to that question", said Maria, putting her arm back around Richard's shoulders.

"How did you and the cabin get out of the Deep Void and back into the Shroud again?" asked Richard.

"I don't know", replied Maria. "With magic, maybe? Just listen to me now, I'll sing to you." She began to sing a haunting lullaby; Richard didn't recognise it, but the tune was soothing and the words comforting. He stopped crying and lay his head on the older girl's lap.

"I'm hungry", he murmured, growing sleepy as he continued to listen to the pretty song.

Maria finished singing and gently stroked his head. "I know Fay, but remember what I told you. You must not eat the food. Those monsters may forget about you if you hide in here and keep quiet. Eating something will turn you into ghost food for that ogress. Almost everyone who has taken the food becomes pale and they get eaten. Well…I remember a boy I met. It didn't work on him. He ate some, but he was different somehow. You though…you must not eat anything."

Richard nodded. "I won't forget", he whispered, his eyes beginning to close.

BANG

The front door swung open and crashed against the wall beside it. Richard bolted upright, his heart pounding wildly in his slight frame. He knew the sound could only mean one thing…she was back. An unintelligible grunt from the huge creature which eased itself through the door sent a shiver down Richard's spine. To him, as a small child, this monster was enormous. She must have been at least eight foot tall, and barely fitted through the door, having to stoop with her shoulders hunched over. As far as Richard was concerned though, she could have been a hundred feet tall. This massive charcoal-skinned ogre of a woman, if you could call her that, with her unsettling ape-like features and long straggly hair, bared her yellowing half-broken teeth as she peered out of her beady eyes, and reached for something on her back. Richard knew what it was; a large wicker basket. He remembered the uncomfortable terrifying ride he had taken in that same basket not long ago. 'Or *was* it a long time ago? Maria said time is different in this place. Maybe I've been here for ages but just can't tell', he thought. He reached for Maria's hand and she squeezed it tightly.

A muffled cry came from within the basket, and Richard caught his breath. 'Oh no,' he thought, 'there's somebody inside it'. A wave of fear welled up in his stomach, and he had to clamp his free hand over his mouth to prevent himself from crying out. 'Maybe the giant monster-lady will forget I'm here if I keep quiet', he thought. 'Mommy and daddy will rescue me soon, as long as I keep quiet right now.'

Dzunukwa swung the basket clumsily around to her front and unstrapped it. The screams from inside had dulled to pitiful whimpers. Richard put his fingers in his ears but he could still hear them. Tipping up the basket, the huge monstrous woman deposited its contents onto the floor. It was a little boy, much smaller than him. The boy's dark curly hair was dishevelled and his cheeks tear-stained and dirty.

"Oh the poor little thing, he only looks about two, or maybe younger", whispered Maria turning pale. "Bakwas and Dzunukwa don't usually bring children that young here."

"Why not?" whispered Richard, almost too terrified to breathe in case Dzunukwa should look at him. Thankfully at the moment her attention seemed to be focused on the boy.

"Maybe it's because very young children are normally with an adult", replied Maria. "He must have wandered away from his parents."

Richard felt his breathing rate beginning to increase as a wild fear rose inside him. "What's she going to do with him?" he asked. "Do you think his mommy will find him here?"

Maria shook her head. "I don't think so. If he eats the food, his spirit will belong to this land, and Dzunukwa will eat him."

Richard's eyes grew large. "Eat him?" he squeaked. He realised too late how loudly he'd spoken, and clamped his hand over his mouth. To his dismay, the giant woman looked up and stared directly in his direction.

"Oh no, she's seen me", squealed Richard. He dived behind Maria in terror, his little body trembling. He began desperately singing the song he'd just heard from Maria in an attempt to calm himself down, but found he couldn't remember the lyrics properly, and the tune didn't sound right either.

"Shhh!" hushed Maria, flapping her arm behind her back at Richard. "Be quiet!"

"I *am* being quiet", said Richard, his voice getting higher and squeakier the more frightened he became.

"No you're not!" whispered Maria with urgency.

Richard began to cry; loud terrified sobs erupted from him as if a dam had broken, and although he hadn't meant to make such a racket, he couldn't help himself. "I don't want her to eat me", he wailed. Dzunukwa let out a roar of anger and began to stomp towards the cage. Even through his cries, Richard could hear the loud thuds approaching from the far side of the room.

"Oh Fay, you've vexed her. This is really not good", chided Maria, her voice shaking.

"W…w…what does vexed mean?" sobbed Richard.

Maria didn't get the opportunity to respond, as Dzunukwa reached the cage and began fumbling with the lock. She let out a few angry mono-syllabic utterances, which sounded nothing like any language Richard had heard before.

"Do you want me to clean the house for you?" Maria asked with a fake smile plastered on her face, reaching her hand bravely through the bars towards Dzunukwa. "How about the windows? I could polish them", she carried on, babbling wildly. Dzunukwa swatted the girl's hand away and continued to fiddle with the cage's padlock.

"Maria don't let her eat me!" Richard screamed. The lock sprang open; the Neanderthal-like woman yanked the door ajar and stuck her hand in through the opening. Richard shuffled backwards until his back was pressed against the furthest corner of the cage, as far from Dzunukwa as he could manage.

The creature's hand felt around the inside of the cage, whilst her disfigured face peered through the bars from the outside. She had terrible hand-eye co-ordination and kept grabbing hold of Maria by mistake, then smacking her around the head when she realised she'd got the wrong person. A clatter from elsewhere in the room caused Dzunukwa to pull her hand back out of the cage, and she clumsily turned to look at the source of the commotion. The little boy had wandered over to a cupboard and was attempting to climb inside, knocking over multiple pots and dishes in the process. "Mama. Want mama", he whimpered. Dzunukwa snorted and lurched towards the storage unit, distracted by the toddler.

Richard looked at the cage door, which, in her haste to reach the small boy, Dzunukwa had forgotten to close. 'Mommy always tells me to stay in one place if I get lost,' he thought, 'but I don't think this is the same as being lost'. Seizing the opportunity, Richard grabbed Maria and hugged her, then bolted out of the cage and raced towards the front door. It was closed, and the handle was large and stiff; it was difficult for Richard to pull it down, as Fay's little hands were not very strong.

"Fay! Hurry!" yelled Maria. Richard turned back to look at the older girl, who was squeezing herself through the cage opening, and gesturing wildly at the far side of the room. He flicked his head the other way to see what she was pointing to, and saw to his horror that Dzunukwa had spotted him. The ogress grimaced horribly and took one step towards the front door. Richard screamed and began desperately jiggling the handle, his heart pounding wildly. "It won't open!" he shrieked.

Maria shoved her way past a large chair to reach Fay, ducking under Dzunukwa's outstretched arm. The little boy in the cupboard, still with the door ajar, was producing a cacophony of noise, crying at the top of his lungs.

"Help me Maria!" screamed Richard, tears flowing freely.

Dzunukwa shambled closer, shouting again in the same incomprehensible language, interspersed with grunts and growls - more like an animal than a person. Maria made it to the door and grabbed the handle, pulling it down sharply. The door swung open as Dzunukwa reached it, but Richard dived out into the dark mist beyond, avoiding her crooked, dirty, taloned hands as they stretched out for him.

Without looking back, he ran as fast as his little legs could carry him. He could hear the thudding of footsteps chasing him, and the angry bellows of Dzunukwa, but gradually they grew fainter as he put some distance between himself and the lumbering ogress. Eventually, when he was sure he was no longer being followed, he slowed to a stop. He flung himself on the ground lying prostrate, and panted heavily from exhaustion. It took some time, but after a while his heart returned to a more normal pace. He sat up and looked around. 'It looks like a forest,' he thought, trying to figure out where he was, 'but not quite like an ordinary forest. It's all misty.' Shadowy shapes were floating around him, and although he could make out the silhouettes of trees, they didn't seem to be really there. Everything appeared dream-like and not altogether physical. "I want my mommy and daddy", he cried, feeling lost and alone. "Where's my mommy?" He stood up and started to walk aimlessly through the misty forest. The shadows whispered all around him, sending chills down his spine, but wearily he trudged on hoping to find something or someone familiar. He prayed he wasn't unintentionally heading back to Dzunukwa's cabin. 'I want Maria', he thought, sniffling. 'I liked Maria. Why didn't she come with me?'

"Fay." A whisper came from a bush he had just passed. He stopped and turned to look at it.

"Who's there?" he asked fearfully.

"Fay," came the voice again. This time it was louder and had a lilting sing-song quality to it. "I'm here to help you. You look so lost and tired and hungry."

Richard began to cry again, and he nodded. "I'm *really* tired and really hungry", he admitted. "I don't know where I am. I want to go home." He sniffled loudly and wiped the back of his hand over his nose.

"Poor little Fay. Look, this bush has lovely berries growing on it. You should eat a few and have a rest. Afterward, I'll help you find your mommy and daddy."

Richard looked at the bush. Sure enough, delicious-looking ripe berries filled the branches. He didn't know what type they were, but he knew he hadn't seen them before. "Are these berries good to eat?" he asked with hesitation. "Mommy always says we mustn't eat fruits without finding out if they're safe. Some are poisonous you know."

"Of course these ones are good to eat", said the voice. "They're really fresh and sweet. Go ahead child, try one. You'll feel so much better."

Richard scratched his nose. "No...I don't think I should", he said, his stomach rumbling. Something Maria had told him about not eating anything was niggling at the back of his mind.

"You'll never find any as wonderful as these ever again", said the voice, with a slight desperate edge to its tone.

"No, really, my mommy and daddy wouldn't be pleased if I ate strange berries." Richard was beginning to feel nervous of the disembodied voice behind the bush. "Can you come out?" he asked. "I want to see you."

The voice laughed. "I'll come out if you eat some berries, Fay", it said.

Richard felt a shiver of fear running down his spine at the voice's insistence. "No", he shouted, stamping his foot. "Stop telling me to eat berries. I want to go home."

The voice let out a sinister growl. "You are trying my patience", it snarled. The leaves of the bushes rustled, and Richard took a step backwards. As he was seeing the world through the eyes of a six-year-old girl, he didn't understand what it meant to try someone's patience; he did, however, realise he had angered the voice somehow.

"I...I'm sorry", he said in a quiet voice, his bottom lip trembling. "Please will you take me home?"

Suddenly the leaves in front of him parted, and through the misty darkness Richard saw two glowing red eyes and a set of jagged yellowing teeth that grinned at him menacingly, like some sort of terrifying deep sea fish. He screamed and stumbled backwards; he caught the heel of his foot on a fallen stick and fell heavily onto his bottom, landing with a hard painful bump on the bracken. The bushes rustled again, and the red eyes and monstrous smile lurched towards him.

"Just *one* berry", growled the voice; no longer pleasant, it now sounded deep and demonic.

Richard's heart was pounding wildly, and he screamed again, scrambling to his feet. He felt as though he was in a nightmare. Without looking back, he turned and began tearing through the trees, but the thick mist made it impossible for him to see further than two steps ahead. He didn't know if he was running in a straight line, or in circles. His little legs ached and he longed to throw himself down on the ground, but his fear of the red-eyed spirit drove him on. "Mommy," he sobbed, "where are you? Daddy?"

"Daddy's here", came an evil chuckle from behind a tree, just ahead of Richard. Before he could react, a shadowy form in human shape emerged into view. It had a deep black tinge to it, and the red eyes and dagger-like teeth appeared even more petrifying than they had when they were in the bushes. "You think you can escape from me?" He let out a hollow laugh. "I'm the King of Ghosts. You're in my realm, child." He moved closer towards Richard and grinned again. "Come on Fay. Dzunukwa is awaiting your return."

Richard shook his head, his body trembling, as Bakwas approached. He stretched out a black shadowy hand, and Richard squeezed his eyes tightly shut. He waited to feel the hand grabbing hold of him, but nothing happened. The whispers around him had stopped, and he was aware of a sensation of no longer being standing up. He felt as though he was lying on something soft and comfortable. Cautiously, he opened his eyes.

At first he was confused and didn't know where he was, but then he realised he was back in the reservation. "Was that all just a dream?" he said aloud, wondering if it really had all happened. He squeezed his eyes shut again, the visions of Bakwas' cabin still playing in his mind. 'Maria...' he thought. 'That's the girl from my nightmare. She was there when I was a child.' He felt as though the air had all been sucked out of his lungs. 'She's still alive', he realised. 'All those years, and she's still alive.' Not knowing whether to laugh or cry, he blinked a few times rapidly. 'She hasn't aged a day!' He knew now it hadn't been a mere dream. 'How would I have known about Maria if it hadn't been real? I really *was* taken to that cabin when I was a boy. I can't believe I'd suppressed the memory all these years.'

The room didn't look as light as it had done earlier, and he wondered what time it was. In a panic he sat up in a hurry and swung his legs out of the bed. He stood up quickly, perhaps a little too quickly, for he felt light-headed and needed to sit back down again for a few moments to compose himself. 'I wonder why Pat didn't wake me', he thought. 'Hell, that must have been what has happened to Fay. When Pat did the spell linking me to her, we must have still been linked when I went to sleep. That's probably how I was able to see through her eyes and witness everything she is going through.' He stood up again, more carefully this time, and walked towards the door. He left the dormitory and headed towards Pat's house, but as he approached he could hear voices inside. 'I recognise that voice', he thought, straining his ears to hear who it might be.

"Well where is he? I don't believe he's not here. The last time I saw him he was with you. You came to the house last night and then he disappeared, and now I find out he hasn't been to work today." The unmistakable sound of Laura's voice drifted from Pat's house.

Richard groaned inwardly. 'Oh God what's she doing here?'

"I am sorry Laura, but you will not find him here", said Pat. "Perhaps he has gone fishing, I know he likes to take his fishing rod and go into the forest."

"No, I don't think so. You are hiding something."

"Laura, don't be so worried about him. I'm sure Richard is fine.

We have nothing to hide", said Olivia.

"I'm not worried, I'm sure he can take care of himself", said Laura. "The problem is that we are supposed to be going on a trip this evening, and he's missing."

"A trip? Oh how lovely", exclaimed Barbara.

There was a brief pause. "Who are you?" asked Laura. She sounded confused. "Do you know Richard?"

"Who me? Oh no, no no."

"Never heard of him", chimed in Mr. Walker, sounding utterly unconvincing.

Richard groaned again, this time out loud. 'Well, Laura is not going to believe a word of that.' He looked up anxiously at the sky; the sun was not as high as he would've liked which meant that it was getting to late afternoon. 'I wonder how long Laura has been here, because Pat should've woken me up well before now.'

"Come on Pat…Olivia…just tell me where he is. Did he not want to go on the trip tonight? Is that the problem? If he is hiding somewhere, my parents are going to kill him."

Pat let out a short laugh. "Hiding? I do not know what made you think he is hiding. Do not be silly Laura. Richard loves you, and he very much wanted to go on this trip with you tonight. He told me this yesterday."

"So when you left our house last night, Richard was still in bed?" asked Laura. She didn't sound as though she had believed what Pat said.

"Of course Laura. Would you like some greenthread tea?" replied Pat.

Richard rubbed his eyes and stretched his legs. 'Well, I shall have to thank Pat later for lying to cover for me. I know how much he hates lying', thought Richard, feeling grateful for what his friend had done for him. Pat was always very honest, and Richard hated that Laura had put him on the spot like that. 'If only I had the guts to tell her I'm a werewolf', he thought. 'I'm such a coward.'

"No thank you, I just need to find Richard", said Laura.

Richard felt a tickle in his nose. 'Oh hell, no, please don't let me sneeze. This is a very inconvenient time to need to sneeze.' The feeling grew stronger, and Richard tried everything to ensure that he did not make a sound, but despite his best efforts he erupted with the most enormous sneeze which echoed through the entire reservation.

"What was that?" cried Laura. "There's only one person I know who sneezes like that, and it's Richard."

"Richard? No of course not, it is someone else. Do you suppose Richard is the only person in the world who sneezes loudly?" said Olivia.

"Of course I don't", said Laura. "You are all acting very strangely though. You're definitely hiding something. I swear that was Richard; I'm going to have a look."

"Oh no, do not go outside. It was nobody you know."

Pat sounded anxious; Richard thought he'd better get out of the way in case Laura really did decide to look around the reservation. He ran away from Pat's house and hurried to the back of the dormitory, where he found a large stack of crates and positioned himself between them so he would not be discovered. It was just in time too, for no sooner had he settled himself behind them did he hear Pat's front door opening and the distinctive footsteps of Laura walking around the reservation grounds. It was her scent which gave her away more than anything. He knew it like the back of his hand. She always wore the same brand of perfume, and it wafted along with the wind towards his nose.

'This is ridiculous', he thought. 'If she finds me here, I'm going to have an awful time trying to explain why I'm hiding behind these boxes. She will think I'm completely mad, or that I'm avoiding her. The Walkers need me to find Fay, and if I'm still here when it's dark, I won't be much use to anybody. I will be a mindless beast.'

"Richard? Richard, are you here?" shouted Laura.

Richard gritted his teeth. He was trying to make up his mind whether or not to remain hidden, or to reveal himself to Laura and try to make up an excuse as to why Pat had said he wasn't there earlier. After listening to Laura calling for a few more moments, he knew he had to do something. She couldn't stay at the reservation

any longer. Soon it would be dusk, and time was running out for
the little girl in the land of the dead. He waited until Laura had
gone around the corner of a building, then quickly stood up from
his hiding spot and hurried around to the front of the dormitory.
He wanted to try to make his way to the reservation entrance, so
it would appear as though he had just arrived. It seemed more
plausible to attempt to convince Laura that he hadn't already
been there, than trying to think of a reason why nobody seemed
to know where he was previously. Of course he realised it would
mean feigning introductions again with the Walkers in front
of Laura, and he hoped they would be able to pull off a better
performance than they had done earlier. 'With a bit of luck, Laura
might just think they are a little strange', he thought hopefully.
He began to tiptoe in the direction of the reservation entrance. He
kept his highly attuned ears alert to ensure he didn't hear Laura
approaching from any direction. Reaching the entrance he paused
for a moment, then made a rather dramatic show of shouting to
attract attention of nearby residents. "Hello", he called. "Where is
Pat?" he asked loudly "I'm here to see him."

The man who was standing nearest to Richard raised an
eyebrow in astonishment. "But weren't you already here?" he asked,
puzzled.

Richard flapped his hand wildly at the man. "Be quiet", he
hushed. "I don't want anyone to hear you."

A second man close to Richard furrowed his brow. "Are you sure
you're okay, Richard?" he asked. "Should I fetch Pat?"

"Yes please", said Richard. "Be discreet though."

"Have you been drinking, Richard?" asked the first man.

Richard snorted. "No", he said, smiling slightly. "I do need to
speak to Pat though. I think Laura might be here."

"Yes", said the second man, stopping in his tracks as he had
started to walk away. He turned again to face Richard. "She's been
shouting, looking for you."

Richard rubbed his chin. "Yeah, so I heard."

"Richard?" came Laura's shrill voice from across the courtyard.
"Richard? Where the hell have you been? I've been looking

everywhere for you. Pat and Olivia said they hadn't seen you, yet here you are."

Richard walked towards the source of the voice, and saw Laura standing with her arms folded across her chest, glaring accusatorially at Pat and Olivia.

"I don't know what you mean", said Richard. "I've only just arrived here."

"Don't lie to me", said Laura angrily. "You haven't been to work today. I showed up at the supermarket to meet you after work, and your boss said you hadn't turned up. He didn't know where you were. He asked me if you were sick, and said you hadn't phoned in."

Richard scratched the back of his neck awkwardly. "Well, yes, I was feeling ill this morning. I guess I forgot to call in sick. I felt better a little later, so I went to the shops."

"You went shopping?" asked Laura with incredulity. "What on earth possessed you to go to shopping? Don't you think there are more important things, like this trip we are supposed to be going on, than going to the shops? What did you buy anyway?"

"Just some food", said Richard, trying to keep his answer vague. "You know, since I burnt the chicken last night, and we didn't have very much left to eat in the kitchen."

"But we aren't going to be home all weekend", pointed out Laura. "Buying food when there isn't going to be anybody to eat it seems a little strange. Besides, don't you think it would have been helpful to let me know where you were going? And then you seem to have come to the reservation. What are you here for?"

"I wanted to say bye to Pat and Olivia before we go on our trip", said Richard, desperately hoping Laura would stop questioning him. "I'm going to miss them."

Laura raised an eyebrow. "Don't be ridiculous", she said. "We are only going for the weekend."

"I wanted to give Richard some greenthread tea to take with him when you go away this weekend", said Pat. "It is very relaxing, and I thought you would both like it. I rang him this morning and asked him to come and fetch it from the reservation."

"Okay", said Laura doubtfully. "Well, we're going to be late.

Come on Richard, you can see your friends when you get back. My parents will be cross if we don't make the most of the trip they paid so much money for."

Richard gulped. He didn't know what to say to get him out of this situation. He needed her to leave so he could return to The Shroud, to try and rescue Fay from Bakwas and Dzunukwa, but she didn't seem to be leaving without him. "Why don't you go on ahead", he said. "I'll meet you at home in a few minutes. There's something I need to do first."

"No", said Laura. "You and Pat always take far too long together. You will be here talking all night. We have to go now."

"Really, I won't be long", insisted Richard. He looked at Pat, Olivia, and the Walkers, hoping somebody would be able to say something to get rid of Laura.

"In fact," said Olivia, "Richard, Pat, and I, are planning something special for your birthday. We wanted to keep it a surprise, but you insist on staying here, so unfortunately now the cat is out of the bag. However we would like to finish planning without you overhearing, so if you could just give us a few minutes, Richard will rejoin you at home."

"Oh!" said Laura, sounding distinctly more cheerful. "You really shouldn't, I mean, how lovely of you all. Well, we do have to get going, but I suppose a few extra minutes won't hurt. Okay Richard, I'll meet you at home, don't be too long." She turned and headed out of the reservation.

Richard admired her slender form as she walked away from him. He felt incredibly guilty for having lied so blatantly to her face, but he had been put in an impossibly difficult situation. Finally when she was out of sight, he turned to face Pat. "We're going to be longer than a few extra minutes", he said. "I hope she doesn't return to find me."

"We won't be here even if she does," said Mr. Walker, "we'll be in the forest, where the cabin is supposed to be".

"That's true," agreed Richard, "but Laura is very resourceful. I wouldn't put it past her searching the forest for me if she discovers I'm not at the reservation and I haven't returned home."

"We must hurry," said Pat, "it is the full moon tonight, and Richard, you will soon be a werewolf beast".

"I am painfully aware of that", said Richard.

"What are we waiting for?" asked Barbara, beginning to head towards the reservation entrance. "We have to find Fay."

"I was meaning to tell you...I had a bad dream just now", said Richard, his mind replaying the events he had seen in his nightmare.

"Dreams are often messages from the spirits", said Olivia. "What did you dream about?"

"I don't think this was a message from the spirits", said Richard. "I think the spell Pat performed linked me to the little girl. I appeared to be seeing through her eyes."

Barbara stopped and turned to face Richard. "Did you say you saw through our daughters eyes?"

Richard nodded. "Yes", he said. "The good news is she is still alive."

Barbara clasped her hand to her heart and a slow smile began to spread across her face. "Oh thank God", she gasped aloud. "I can't tell you what a relief that is."

"What's the bad news?" asked Mr. Walker.

Richard winced. "Dzunukwa and Bakwas are pretty scary", he admitted. "Bakwas was trying to get your daughter to eat some berries, but she was sensible enough to refuse."

"We always told her not to eat unusual fruits", said Barbara. "She also wouldn't be likely to eat anything offered by a stranger."

Richard shuddered, remembering the glowing red eyes and terrifying teeth. "This is no ordinary stranger. Bakwas is monstrous", he said. "Nobody in their right mind would accept anything from him once they see what he really looks like. At first though he sounded quite charming, but Fay wasn't fooled."

Mr Walker looked pleased. "She always was sensible", he said.

"She should not have run into the forest in the first place", said Pat. "She should have stayed at your house."

Barbara grimaced. "Yes, of course, but she's only a child. Children make mistakes."

It was at that moment Richard realised Kingfisher was not with the group. "Where's King?" he asked, looking around. "I haven't seen him since I woke up."

"Good point," said Olivia, "he said he was going to do something while you slept. Perhaps we ought to get him."

"Yes," said Pat, "but we must remember, Richard does not have very long as a human. We have to ensure Fay has been rescued before midnight, and that Richard is somewhere safe, where he will not harm anyone when he changes into a beast."

Olivia nodded. "I will go and see if I can find him. If I'm not back in a few minutes, start making your way through the forest toward the spot where the cabin is. We will meet you there."

"Okay," said Pat, "try not to be long".

Olivia began walking away from the group. Richard watched her for a moment, then made his way out of the reservation, with Pat and the Walkers close behind him. "I think I can remember the way to Bakwas' cabin", said Richard. "It shouldn't be too difficult for me to pick up the scent, and besides, I'm pretty good at memorising directions."

"Yes," said Pat, "I can remember also. We Navajo are also very good at tracking and directions."

"Of course", said Richard. He knew this to be true. At university, Pat had always been the one to direct new students to their classes, even though he had only been there for a short time himself. "Well, if I get lost, I guess we can rely on you", he said with a grin.

"Do not be silly Richard," said Pat, "you will not get lost".

"I know, I was only joking", replied Richard.

"This is no time for jokes", said Mr. Walker. "This is a very serious situation."

"I'm sorry", said Richard. "I didn't mean to upset you. I will get your daughter back, I promise."

Barbara reached over to Richard and grabbed his hand. "She means everything to us", she said, sounding anguished.

"Yes, I'm sure", said Richard. "She seems like a nice kid."

"I can't believe you saw her", said Mr. Walker.

"I didn't *exactly* see her", said Richard. "It was as though I...it's hard to explain…I *was* her."

Barbara frowned. "I'm still not sure I understand," she said, "but if she is still alive that gives me hope. Thank you Richard."

Richard shook off Barbara's hand from his own in order to push aside some branches which were hanging in front of him. "She wasn't alone", he said. "There were other children there too."

"More of them?" said Pat. "How many?"

"Two, as far as I could see", replied Richard. "A little boy, he looked about two, and…" he hesitated, "a girl. She's older than Fay, around twelve or thirteen."

"Oh no," exclaimed Barbara, "do you suppose these children have gone missing recently?"

"I do not know", said Pat. "I have not seen a newspaper for many weeks."

"The older girl had been there for a while", said Richard. "She's Bakwas and Dzunukwa's servant."

"Servant?" queried Pat. "I have never heard of Bakwas and Dzunukwa having a servant. This is not in any legends."

Richard shrugged, trying to seem nonchalant. "Perhaps the legends don't tell us everything we need to know."

"It is not impossible they may have taken a servant at a later time", said Pat. "They are known for taking people to the land of the dead. They may have acquired a servant at some point."

"I have to save her", said Richard firmly.

Pat stared at Richard. "The boy as well?" he queried.

"Oh…yeah…of course…" stammered Richard. He didn't want to have to explain why it meant so much to him that he save Maria in particular.

The group fell into a silence, as they continued to traipse through the forest.

CHAPTER EIGHT

Laura swore under her breath as her foot caught on a root and she stumbled. 'Having to go home on my own isn't exactly convenient', she thought, feeling cross. Her pleasure at hearing that Richard was planning something for her birthday was quickly giving way to irritation when she realised he was essentially leaving her to prepare for their weekend away all by herself. 'My birthday isn't until after the wedding. Why can't this wait?' Her mind flicked back to the couple at the reservation with Pat. 'I didn't recognise them, but they were acting very suspiciously when I asked about Richard', she thought. 'That woman was pretty. I wonder if…' she shook her head, dismissing her doubts. 'Don't be silly. She looked at least a few years older than Richard…more like mid thirties. She could have been ten years older! Surely Richard wouldn't…' Her train of thought tailed off. 'No, that's ridiculous. He must have been just planning my birthday as he said. Then again, I don't know that woman, so what does she have to do with my birthday preparations?'

"You look as though there's a lot on your mind", came a male voice from behind her.

Laura let out a little scream and jumped, clutching her hand to her heart. She turned to see a man in jeans and a t-shirt behind her. He appeared to be in his early to mid forties; a Native American. His hair was long and untamed, and he stared at her with piercing eyes. Normally she wasn't attracted to someone fifteen to twenty years older than her, but he had such chiselled handsome features and rugged good looks that she couldn't help feeling her cheeks begin to redden. "Oh, you startled me", she said, her heart pounding.

"Sorry", the man replied with a grin. "I was just passing by."

"I didn't hear you", admitted Laura.

The man smiled again. "I'm quiet." He stuck out his right hand. "My name is Ahiga."

Laura hesitated for a moment, then took his hand and shook it. "I'm Laura", she replied.

"Pretty name", Ahiga said with a wink.

Laura felt herself blush again. 'Surely he's not flirting with me', she thought. "What are you doing out here in the forest?" she asked, trying to make small talk with the attractive stranger.

Ahiga shrugged. "I don't live far from here." He stuck his hand into the pocket of his jeans and pulled out a small silver flask. "Are you thirsty?" he asked.

Laura wrinkled her nose and eyed the flask with suspicion. "What is it?"

"Something to whet the whistle", Ahiga replied. "You look like you have a lot on your mind; I think this will help."

Laura took the offered flask, unscrewed the lid, and sniffed. It smelled like whiskey and strawberries. Tentatively, she put the bottle rim to her lips and took a sip. "Oh that is rather nice", she said in surprise.

"One of my favourites", said Ahiga. "Do you mind if I walk with you awhile?" he asked. "It seems as though we are heading in the same direction."

Laura shrugged. She didn't mind at all if Ahiga wanted to walk with her. It was pleasant to have some company. They set off through the forest once again, and she found her thoughts beginning to drift. What had Richard really been up to at the reservation? The more she thought about it the more she was sure she had caught a glimpse of him. At first the memory was fuzzy, but the further she walked, the stronger the recollection became. She could see in her mind's eye as clear as day, the naked body of her fiancé writhing on the ground with the woman she had later seen with Pat and Olivia. She could vividly hear their groans of passion. 'The bastard', she thought, seething with rage. 'How could he do this to me just before our wedding?' She stopped walking, trying to clear her head. 'Am I just imagining this?' she thought, not wanting to believe it. 'No, he did do this, I remember it so clearly.'

"Are you okay?" asked Ahiga.

"Oh", said Laura. She had almost forgotten she was not alone. "Yes…well, no, not really." She felt uncomfortable revealing her thoughts to a complete stranger.

"I am a good listener", said Ahiga, offering her the flask again. Laura grabbed it without a second thought, and gulped down several large mouthfuls of the strawberry flavoured drink.

At once her mind flicked back again to the memory of the reservation. Richard was thrusting himself into that other woman, kissing her passionately. He ran his lips down to her breasts. Laura was trembling, watching them entangled together. Her fury boiled into a mixture of despair, desperation, rage, and…something else. Then she realised what it was; she was incredibly turned on. She hated Richard for cheating on her, but the memory of two people having sex like that was stirring a desire inside her.

"You can see him with her, can't you?" whispered a voice in her ear. Laura moaned softly as Ahiga's lips skimmed over her hair. "You can see them both, their flesh entwined. He fucked her, Laura. You saw it, didn't you?"

Laura nodded. She felt intoxicated, and she could only see Richard and the other woman. The forest was just a blur around her, but the memory was crystal clear.

"How does it make you feel?" whispered Ahiga. He trailed one finger along her jaw-line and ran it lightly down her neck.

"He's an asshole", slurred Laura. "We are meant to be getting married."

"You could always get your own back", murmured Ahiga. "That way you'd be even." He slipped his hand under the bottom of her blouse, and Laura made no move to push him away. She could feel her skin tingling with pleasure at his touch, and although a fleeting doubt sprang into her mind, the vision of Richard pounding himself into that woman was so strong, that she quickly dispelled her guilt.

'He didn't hesitate to screw someone else', she thought bitterly, her body responding to Ahiga as he began to unbutton her blouse. She didn't even care that they were on the path through the forest where anyone could have walked past. Ahiga unfastened the last button and Laura flung her blouse to the ground. She didn't give him chance to take off her bra; she did it herself, dropping it carelessly. Ahiga's mouth immediately found her nipples and he flicked his tongue over them, causing tingles to run through her body. 'No, this is wrong', a tiny voice inside her shouted, but she inwardly told it to quieten down. "I want you to do to me what he did to her", she said aloud, her voice sounding thick and strange to her own ears.

Ahiga handed Laura the flask again, and she giggled, taking it from him. Without hesitation she downed the remainder of the liquid. All her rage towards her fiancé for sleeping with another woman intensified, and with it, the desire to channel that anger into wild crazy sex with this handsome stranger. She leant back, and could physically feel her clitoris pulsating. As if by instinct she thrust her hips towards him, and he grabbed hold of her trousers, pulling them down and off her legs. Before Laura even had time to collect her thoughts, Ahiga had taken her underwear in his teeth and torn them from her body. Laura gasped with delight and reached out to him.

"We'll make him suffer", growled Ahiga, stepping back and whipping off his own clothes, and pulling Laura towards him. Without saying another word, he hoisted her up and she wrapped her legs around him. He pushed her back against a tree, penetrating her with one swift hard motion. Laura let out a moan as Ahiga began thrusting her up and down on him. She felt him deep inside her, and she clutched onto his shoulders, running her fingers through his long hair. She could feel her orgasm building up, and she could tell from Ahiga's panting that he was not far behind her. Finally she reached her peak, and Laura screamed as she climaxed, her body sending waves of explosive pleasure through her. Ahiga groaned loudly and rammed himself inside her hard before weakly dropping them both to the ground, where they lay panting.

"I've never been so impulsive", said Laura, her thoughts still lingering on the memory of Richard cheating on her. As she remained on her back on the bracken, the day growing later and the shadows dabbling the forest through the canopy of leaves above her head, something started to niggle her. "How did you know what I was thinking about?" she asked, realising it didn't make sense.

"I could just tell", replied Ahiga vaguely. He sat up and began pulling on his clothes.

Laura frowned, her mind suddenly clouded by confusion. Already her recollection of Richard with the other woman had started to fade, and she felt a twinge of remorse. "What if...what if I was mistaken", she said. "What if he didn't actually do anything wrong. Maybe I was mistaken." 'Did I see him with her? I don't know, I can't remember', she thought, thoroughly perplexed.

"You enjoyed what we just did, so just don't worry about it", soothed Ahiga. "You don't need him anyway. You need a real man like me."

Laura bit her lip and felt as though she was going to cry. "But what do I do now? I can't go home. I've just had sex with you! What if I was mistaken, and Richard didn't cheat on me? Oh God, what have I done?"

Ahiga handed over her clothes. Laura took them from him, sat up, and quickly put them back on. "I can't believe we did that", she said, her thoughts whirling.

"It was good though, wasn't it?" Ahiga said, with a wink.

Laura felt her face turn red. "That is not the point", she said. "I'm engaged."

"That didn't stop you a few minutes ago", pointed out Ahiga. "Anyway, he was with another woman."

"Yes..." began Laura, "but...was he? I'm not sure now...I feel really confused." The image of Richard sliding his body over that other woman no longer seemed clear. It was as though she had woken up from a dream, which was slipping away. 'Why did I think I had seen him doing that?' wondered Laura. 'He wouldn't do something like that to me, I am sure of it. I didn't really see him, did I?' She shook her head, trying to figure out what was real and what was not.

"Just come with me; I don't live too far from here. You said it yourself, you can't really go home now after this. Besides, I'm pretty good company", said Ahiga, smiling. He held out his hand to Laura.

Laura raised an eyebrow. 'I can't go with him', she thought. 'He's a complete stranger.'

Ahiga looked at her and smiled again. He really did have a perfect smile as far as Laura was concerned. "You're hesitant, I can see that", he said. "If you're worried about the fact that we barely know each other, I think we are a little past that by now, don't you?"

Laura had to admit he had a point. This was hardly a time to be shy; after all, they had just been intimate. "I think perhaps I had better just face the music", she replied. She wanted nothing less than to go home, and have to confess to Richard what she had done, but she felt as though it was the appropriate thing to do.

Ahiga gave a short laugh. "Maybe the right thing is you leaving that guy of yours, and coming with me."

Laura hesitated for just a moment longer, then impulsively took Ahiga's hand. 'What am I doing?' she thought. Deep down though, she knew why she was going with him. The thought of facing her fiancé was too much to bear. Her stomach churned as she imagined what the expression on his face would look like - the hurt from learning of her betrayal would be etched into his features. She could picture it now, and she didn't want to see the real thing. "I must have been mistaken", she said. "I don't think he did cheat on me."

"You still deserve a proper man like me", said Ahiga. He began to walk through the forest. Laura tagged along, her hand still being held by Ahiga's. She had no idea where they were going, only that Ahiga had said he lived quite close. On and on they walked until they neared the edge of town. "We're nearly there", said Ahiga. Laura was a little surprised. She thought she had seen almost everybody in that small town at one point or another, and she definitely would have noticed someone like Ahiga. To her puzzlement though, they didn't turn to follow the path into town, but rather tailed off in the opposite direction.

"Do you live in the forest itself?" asked Laura.

Ahiga nodded. "Yes, my camp is just up ahead."

'Camp?' thought Laura feeling a little worried. 'Does that mean he's in some kind of cult or commune?' "Do you mean a reservation?" she queried.

Ahiga laughed. "No, not exactly. Not an official reservation. We're just a gathering of...friends...who live together. It is better that way."

Laura wasn't sure she liked the way he hesitated when he said friends, but she decided to take him at his word, and continued to walk with him towards his camp. Before long, she caught sight of a group of tents assembled in a clearing in the forest. "Is this where you live?" she asked, feeling nervous.

Ahiga nodded. "Come and meet the others", he said. He smiled, a strange sort of smile. "I think you're going to like it here."

'What does he mean by that?' thought Laura. 'It is not as though I'm going to be staying for very long.' "Maybe this was a bad idea", she said. "I should probably go home."

Ahiga clutched her hand tightly. "Oh no, I insist you stay for a while. It is the least I can do, after..." he grinned. "Well, saying that, you enjoyed it as much as I did."

Laura's stomach flipped over. The annoying thing was that Ahiga was right. She *had* enjoyed it, but she didn't want to admit it. 'It was a mistake', she thought. 'I love Richard.' Still, there was something about Ahiga that intrigued her.

They entered the campsite, and as they walked between the tents, Laura saw what appeared to be a long string washing line, erected high into the air between two trees. Hanging from the line were many animal skins of different shapes and sizes. Some appeared to be wolf skins, some bear, others small creatures like rabbits and badgers.

"What an earth do you need all those skins for?" asked Laura.

"You'll see in due time", replied Ahiga mysteriously.

They walked further into the campsite and a few Native Americans began to emerge from the tents. One or two of them approached Ahiga and Laura and bowed.

'I wonder if Ahiga is their leader or something', thought Laura.

"This is Laura", said Ahiga to the other men and women, gesturing to her beside him.

'I don't remember telling him my name', thought Laura, feeling uneasy.

"We didn't think you were going to bring her here", said one of the men, looking Laura up-and-down.

Laura took a step backwards self-consciously. 'What does he mean?' she wondered. "Ahiga and I have only just met", she said, confused why the others in the campsite were exchanging conspiratorial smiles and nudging each other. 'Haven't they ever had someone new visit the camp?' she thought, fiddling with her hair.

"We will be in my tent", snapped Ahiga, sounding angry all of a sudden. "Be sure not to disturb us." He took hold of Laura's hand and began striding purposefully through the campsite, towards the far side, where a large red tent stood alone. It was significantly bigger than any of the other tents in the campsite.

'I was right', thought Laura. 'He must be the leader of them, otherwise his tent wouldn't be so enormous.'

Ahiga bent down, unzipped the tent, and lifted up the canvas so Laura could enter. "After you", he said. It would have been gallant of him, if he didn't have a slight dangerous edge to his tone of voice which Laura found unnerving. Ahiga must have sensed her unease and he relaxed his face. "We'll just talk", he said.

Laura bit her bottom lip, but nodded, and ducked to enter. Inside there was a double mattress and plenty of plump cushions. She gingerly sat down on the edge of the mattress. "This is a nice tent", she said, feeling awkward.

Ahiga reached for a glass bottle on the floor at the side of the mattress. He opened the lid, and Laura caught the unmistakeable whiff of whiskey with strawberries. 'It's the same drink he had in his flask', she realised.

"Would you like another drink?" asked Ahiga, offering her the bottle.

Laura shook her head. "No, thank you", she said, trying to be polite.

Ahiga frowned; a sudden expression of wounded hurt on his face. "I thought you liked it", he said. "Go on, just a small one. It'll take your mind off things."

Laura wasn't sure what to say. She didn't want to offend him so she reached for the bottle. "Just a small drink then", she said, trying to be polite. She lifted it to her lips and took a sip. No sooner had the liquid slid down her throat did it all come flooding back to her. The reason she was there in the first place was because of Richard's infidelity.

"What are you thinking about?" prompted Ahiga. "Your fiancé?"

Laura nodded. "I *did* see him with another woman. I definitely did", she said adamantly. The memory of them together filled her mind like a pornographic movie, and her heart began beating faster.

"Do you feel a little dizzy?" asked Ahiga, sounding concerned. His voice sounded smooth and seductive, and hazy, as though she were in a dream. "Lie back if you like."

Laura allowed herself to lean back against the cushions. Ahiga pressed his mouth against hers and kissed her fiercely. She responded in turn; her lips searching for his as though in desperation. He reached down and unbuttoned her trousers, sliding one hand down into them. Laura arched her back and spread her legs apart, wanting him to take her again.

Suddenly, a loud cough interrupted them. Abruptly, Ahiga pulled his hand away and leapt to his feet. "I said nobody was to disturb us", he shouted, sounding enraged.

"I am sorry Ahiga, but we need to speak to you about an urgent matter", said a male voice. Laura couldn't see who it was that had spoken, but she was cross with them for barging in like that. Her body was still screaming for Ahiga to bring her to climax again.

"Can't it wait?" she slurred, reaching for Ahiga's hand. "Richard deserves to have me sleep with you again, the cheating bastard."

Ahiga let out a groan. "Just...hold that thought. I'll be right back", he said, pulling his hand away and standing up. In two strides he had left the tent. Laura remained on the mattress, her trousers still unbuttoned and her frustration level at a peak, her memories of Richard's unfaithfulness dominating her every thought.

CHAPTER NINE

Richard lifted his head and sniffed the air, trying to ascertain whether or not Olivia and Kingfisher might be returning, but he could not catch their scent. 'Perhaps Olivia hasn't found him yet', he thought. 'It is a bit strange. I wouldn't have thought Kingfisher would be likely to go missing at a time like this.'

It took some time but eventually they reached the place where they had been earlier. Richard surveyed the area; there was nothing to suggest a cabin was here at all.

"I want to go with you", said Mr. Walker. "There must be a way. You have no magical abilities; you might need my help."

Pat shook his head. "I do not think there is a way for you to join Richard in the land of the dead. He will manage. I do not expect him to fight anybody. He will simply retrieve your daughter and bring her back with him."

"You make it sound so easy", said Richard, raising his eyebrow. "You haven't seen the things I've seen."

Barbara turned pale. "Don't say things like that", she said, imploringly. "Just tell me you will be able to do it."

"Of course I'll be able to do it", reassured Richard, hoping he was right.

"You should begin," said Pat, "we will not wait for Olivia and Kingfisher. Time is of the essence. We do not know how long it will take them to arrive."

Richard took a deep breath. He sat down on the bracken, cross legged, and closed his eyes. He heard Pat and the Walkers sit themselves down on the floor beside him. 'Focus Richard', he told himself. 'That little girl is depending on you. You have to get to the land of the dead.' He tried to clear his mind of everything, and concentrated on the most powerful emotions he could summon up. He remembered the terror the little girl had felt when she had been chased by Bakwas. That fear coursed through him now like a wave. A shiver ran down his spine and his stomach began to churn. That's when he began to hear them; subtle at first but then definitely audible, whispers all around him.

'It's working', he thought, whilst still trying to maintain the sense of fear so he wouldn't return to the real world yet. The whispers grew louder, although he still couldn't make out what they were saying. He wondered if that was because their conversation was not directed at him. He opened his eyes and looked around. Pat and the Walkers were no longer visible, but he could tell he was still in the forest. The trees didn't seem real and were shrouded with thick mist. Directly in front of him was a large wooden cabin; the same one he had seen previously. He shuddered. He hated coming to the land of the dead; it was so creepy. What made it even worse was the memory of what was inside that cabin. It looked dark and ominous. He looked around for somewhere to hide, for he wanted to observe it first for a few moments before approaching. There were plenty of trees but they seemed only semi-opaque, so he wasn't sure they were going to be much use to him. Still, he didn't think he had much of a choice, as there was nowhere else. As quietly as possibly he tiptoed towards a nearby tree and positioned himself behind it, hoping he wouldn't be visible through the mist. He fixed his gaze on the cabin, wondering if anyone, or anything, would emerge from it.

He didn't have to wait for very long, for the unmistakable sound of a child screaming reached his ears. His heart began to pound wildly, but it was almost comforting in a place like this to be able to hear and feel his own heartbeat. 'Oh my God, was that Fay?' he thought in a panic. Without hesitating, he emerged from his hiding place and hurried over to the cabin. The screaming continued, and he realised he was hearing not one voice, but two. 'I am coming Fay', he thought, full of determination.

Gingerly, he crept to the cabin and crouched underneath the windowsill. The screams were much louder, almost deafening, and he was sure he could hear the sound of eating. Then he heard

a little boy's voice. "Want Mama! Hurt Me! Hurt me!" the voice
screamed and sobbed, then stopped. The slurps and disgusting
guzzling noises coming from inside the cabin churned his stomach.
He remembered that sound. The image of a little boy floated into
his mind's eye; the face of his friend Thomas. The last time he'd
heard such a vile sound was when Thomas was being eaten alive by
Bakwas and Dzunukwa. Richard gritted his teeth, carefully stood
up, and peeked in through the window. The sight inside the room
was more than he had prepared for, and he had to crouch back
down almost instantly for he feared he would be sick. He closed
his eyes tightly shut, but he still couldn't escape the awful scene he
had just witnessed, and it replayed itself over and over in his mind.
Dzunukwa had been sitting at a large wooden table, the same one
Richard had seen before. Beside the table, exactly as there had been
when he was there as a young boy, a large pile of bones littered the
floor. On the table itself in front of Dzunukwa were various body
parts. All were very small, and he knew they had belonged to the
toddler he had seen in his dream. 'Oh my God, the poor little boy.'
It took all Richard's willpower to prevent himself from heaving and
throwing up outside the window, knowing he had just witnessed
this small boy's final breath. He knew he had to remain silent if he
didn't want to lose any chance of being able to rescue Fay. Steeling
himself for what he knew he would see, once again he rose and
peered through the pane. The ogre was making short work of the
meal in front of her, and the two girls, Fay and Maria, were in the
same cage he had seen before; the same one he'd been trapped
inside himself as a child so many years ago. Presumably Bakwas
had simply taken Fay back to the cabin after accosting her in the
forest. Richard assumed she must have still not eaten any berries,
as she was still alive.

'How the hell am I going to get in there to rescue Fay?' he
thought. 'I can't leave the other girl either. I don't know why she
hasn't tried to escape yet, or why she's being held as a slave, but
there's no way I'm leaving her here with those two monsters.'
Fay was crying and Maria had her arm around the little girl.
The terrifying ogress in the middle of the room didn't pay them

very much attention; she was far too occupied with what she was eating. Every now and again she emitted a disgusting sounding belch, as she continued to chew on morsels of human flesh. A foul stench wafted out from the room. It smelled like rotting corpses and fermenting mouldy meat. Richard clamped his hand over his mouth to prevent himself from vomiting. 'I can't stay here all night, I haven't the time', he thought. 'I need to find a way into the cabin without being noticed.'

He knew the front door of the cabin led directly to Dzunukwa. 'That's not very convenient', he thought. He slowly began to make his way around to the back, trying to determine if there might be an alternate entrance. It was dark at the rear of the building, and he pressed his nose up against a window-pane to see inside. Even with his heightened vision he couldn't see very clearly. The room was not lit, but he could just make out a large wooden door at the far side. 'Hmmm...perhaps I could get this window open somehow, and climb in', he thought. Noticing there was an adjacent window, he decided to take a look through it, in case he spotted something he might have missed. To his astonishment, as he approached, he heard a faint whimpering sound from inside the room. 'Another kidnapped child?' he wondered. 'Why are they being kept here instead of in the cage at the front with the two girls?' He pushed the window cautiously. He didn't really expect anything to happen, but to his surprise it began to open. 'This is a little too easy', he thought warily. 'If this window is open, why didn't the kids try to escape?' He looked down at his fingertips, and decided, experimentally, to extract his claws. He had never attempted any sort of transformation, not even a partial one, whilst in the land of the dead before, so he didn't know what would happen. To his relief, his claws extended from his hands fairly effortlessly, but there was an unusual tingling sensation which he had never felt before. 'It doesn't feel like that when I extract my claws normally', he thought, feeling a little worried. 'I hope I don't have to change into a wolf while I am here, I don't think it would be a good idea.' The window was quite high off the ground, so he sank his claws into the log wall and hoisted himself up. Swinging his legs through the opening, he dislodged his grip and landed softly on his feet in the room. It was pitch black inside; the mist from the forest was now seeping in. He found it very difficult to distinguish any objects. The whimpering sound he had heard was still continuing from the far corner. "Hello?" whispered Richard, feeling nervous. "I won't hurt you, I'm a friend. What's your name?" The whimpering stopped for a moment, and Richard thought he might have frightened the child. "Really," he carried on, "I'm here to help". He began to make his way to the far side of the room where he believed the sound had originated from. The room remained silent as he took his first two steps, but then it all changed. Instead of whimpering, a half squealing, half grunting noise began. Richard stepped backwards in shock as two glowing red eyes appeared, cutting through the unnatural darkness ahead of him. He stumbled over a loose floor plank, stepping backward and knocking into what could only be described as pans on string, which clattered and banged then fell to the ground with a crash.

Alarmed, he jumped forward, but before he could move any further the door leading to the living room was swung violently open, and the monstrous woman barged straight in. Light from the living room flooded in with her; he could see on her grotesque features a horrible contorted expression of rage. Blood was dripping from her open jaws, which Richard presumed was from the little boy she had been eating. She opened her mouth and bellowed loudly. Dzunukwa lurched unsteadily towards Richard, but another grunt from the corner of the room stopped her in her tracks. She turned her attention away from him and began to sway towards the sound. For the first time, Richard could make out a large rectangular wooden object where the noises had come from. Suddenly all memories of the demonic monstrous babies came flooding back to him. He knew he ought to run away, but he remained frozen to the spot, unable to move. Dzunukwa swung around and stared at him straight in the eye. She opened her foul-smelling mouth and growled sickeningly, drooling onto the floor. She had seemed bigger when he was a boy, but despite the fact he'd grown taller, she was still a good two foot larger than him.

There was an instant when neither of them moved a muscle. They both simply stared at each other, whilst the squalling toddler in the cot continued to whine. It sounded like a pig, for its squeals were interspersed with grunts and growls. A new noise behind him made him jump. Without even turning around, he knew what it was. The second child in the other crib was smacking its chops hungrily. He'd heard that sound before, when the creatures had first caught sight of his best friend Thomas' semi-devoured body on the floor of the cabin, so many years ago. 'Oh shit...what do I do?' he thought. He knew if he stepped backwards, the little monster behind him would clamp its ravenous jaws around him. He could see the door out of the corner of his eye, but dared not make a move towards it. It was the ultimate showdown.

"Is someone there?" a voice called from the next room. It sounded like a young girl, and Richard caught his breath, realising it was Fay.

She began to cry. "Please help me. I want to go home."

Dzunukwa screamed something unintelligible, and turned away from Richard. Someone in the next room let out a shriek of terror. Despite not being close to the girls, Richard could hear their little heartbeats racing. The gormless ogress left her babies in their cribs and charged through the door back into the living room. The girls' shrieks became louder. 'I have to do something', thought Richard in desperation. 'That monster may kill them.' Without hesitation, he ran through the door after Dzunukwa. In one swift motion he leapt as high as he could at her back, and sank his claws into her shoulders. The brute screamed in pain and thrashed around wildly, but Richard clung on for all he was worth. The children in their cage were still wailing pitifully. "Just bear with me girls," Richard grunted, "I'm here to help you". The monster tried to reach around her own back, swatting at him in vain. "You can't get me you dumb bitch", Richard snarled, through gritted teeth.

"Look out!" yelled Maria.

'Look out for what?' thought Richard, in alarm. Dzunukwa lurched violently, and Richard dug his claws into her flesh even deeper to avoid being thrown to the floor. He heard a bang behind him, and a gust of mist and freezing air blew in from the now open front door. Out of the corner of his eye he saw a black shadow entering the cabin. 'Oh hell no,' he gasped inwardly, 'it's Bakwas'. Despite the new threat in the cabin, Richard obstinately refused to let go of Dzunukwa's shoulders.

"He'll eat you!" screamed Fay.

Distracted by the little girl's cry, Richard lost his grip as Dzunukwa spun around violently. His body slammed to the floor and he heard his own bones crunch. "Owww!" he groaned, feeling the wind being knocked out of his lungs. He looked up just in time to see Dzunukwa and Bakwas both bearing down on him. Not knowing what else to do, Richard reacted instinctively and changed into a wolf. Usually, performing this action was instantaneous and easy, but this was different. Although he hadn't any trouble extending his claws, the full body change proved more difficult. It felt as though he had been hit by a train. A massive jolt ricocheted through his solar plexus and he inhaled sharply. 'This must be a side effect of changing while in the land of the dead', he thought, right before passing out.

Richard gradually became aware of someone shaking his arm... except it didn't feel like an arm. "Who's that?" he tried to say, but instead of speaking, he whined. 'Oh, wow, I guess it worked', he thought, struggling to open his eyes. "I'm apparently still alive. That can't be a bad thing."

"Wake up Mister Wolf", came a little girl's voice.

"Fay, you need to stay away from him", said a second girl. "He could be dangerous. My mama was a shape changer too, and she was very dangerous."

"Could she turn into a wolf?" asked Fay.

"Sort of; a scary wolf anyway."

"I don't think this guy is scary", replied Fay. He was here to help us."

Maria snorted. "He didn't manage", she said.

Richard forced his eyes open and struggled to sit up. He was inside the cage with the two girls. Being a large wolf it was a tight fit, and he was pressed up against them like an oversized dog.

"Turn back into a man please", said Maria. "We need to talk to you."

Richard willed his body to change...but nothing happened. 'Wow,' he thought, puzzled, 'I must have really hit my head or something. Maybe I'm distracted.' He tried again, and again, and again. 'Oh my God, I can't turn back.'

"Come on, change back. Bakwas and Dzunukwa will be home soon. They'll try to get you to eat something. You have to hurry; you said you were here to help us", urged Maria.

'I'm trying,' thought Richard, 'can't you see I'm trying?' He attempted it one last time, but to no avail.

Fay looked at the older girl with a puzzled expression. "I don't think he can turn back", she said.

"Well, he managed it before", pointed out Maria. "Saying that," she continued, "things don't work the same way here as they do in the real world".

'This is probably the type of thing my grandfather warned me about', Richard thought. 'Being unable to turn back into a human is going to cause some problems.'

"Who are you?" asked Maria.

"Wolves can't talk", said Fay. "You're older than me, you should know that."

Maria slumped back against the cage bars. "I suppose it doesn't matter anyway", she said, sounding dejected. "He wouldn't have been able to rescue us. Bakwas and Dzunukwa are too powerful."

"He must be pretty powerful himself", said Fay, wrinkling her nose. "After all, he can turn into a wolf."

'What time is it?' thought Richard worriedly. 'I hope it's not near midnight yet, otherwise I'm going to have real problems.' He looked at the girls next to him. 'We're *all* going to have real problems!' The misty moonlight shone in through the cabin window. It looked surreal, as though he was looking through water. 'This is a weird sort of place', he thought, wishing he were back in the real world and not in The Shroud. He gave himself a shake. 'Can't sit around here doing nothing.' Without wasting any more time, Richard began to lean against the cage door, pushing hard with all his might.

"What are you doing?" asked Maria, her eyes wide.

"He's trying to break down the door I think", said Fay. The two girls watched him for a few moments.

Richard strained against the metal bars, but they didn't even budge. 'God, what are these things made of?' he wondered, frustrated. 'Surely I'm strong enough to break a simple cage open? I'm a werewolf!' Still, try as he might it would not yield, not even under his brute strength.

'You're in the land of the dead now', said Maria with a sigh. 'I told you, things are different here. I've been here a long time, I've seen it all.'

'You said you weren't sure if you'd been here a long time', chimed in Fay.

Maria rolled her eyes at the younger girl. 'Well, it seems like I have', she conceded. 'Don't be pedantic.'

'What does that mean?'

Maria sighed again. 'It's what my mama always used to say. Never mind.'

As he continued to push against the cage door, a small unnatural noise from somewhere in the room caught Richard's attention. He pricked up his ears and stopped what he was doing. 'What was that?'

"You have to keep pushing", urged Fay, seemingly oblivious to the sound Richard had heard.

'She doesn't have my sense of hearing', realised Richard. He gave a tiny whine.

"I think he's heard something", said Maria. "Look at his ears."

Richard wasn't sure what the sound could be. He lifted his nose up and took deep inhalation of air, but the scent was all muddled. The thick fog in the land of the dead created a sort of musky layer around any aromas, and Richard found it hard to differentiate between scents. He wanted to be able to call out, to ask if someone was there, but stuck as a wolf, all he could do was whine.

"There, there", said Fay, stroking his head. "What's the matter?"

"Stop stroking him", said Maria. "He probably doesn't like it."

Richard was too concerned with the noise he had heard to pay much attention to the girls. He pulled away from Fay, and shuffled closer to where the noise had come from. Suddenly, a particularly pungent waft of aroma headed towards him, and he instantly realised what it was. 'Oh my God,' he thought, shocked, 'it's a human being'.

CHAPTER TEN

Before Richard's eyes, a shape started to materialise in the living room. At first it was shadowy and ghost-like, but then it became more visible, until at last a man was standing in the room. He didn't look particularly threatening. He was in his mid-twenties, a little unkempt, but generally Richard had the feeling he wasn't there to harm them. His expression was sad and anxious.

Maria glanced down at Richard with a nervous look in her eye. "Is that someone you know?" she asked, her voice shaking a little. Richard felt sorry for the girls, and realised any stranger must seem like a threat. He nuzzled Maria's leg with his nose, and she squealed a little, wiping away the dampness with her hand. "Stop it", she complained. "Is this your friend?"

Richard shook his head. Maria looked warily at the man.

"Me name's James, or Jim, either'll do", said the man, with a thick rural dialect from somewhere in England. He took one step towards the cage. "I'm lookin' for me wife's nephew. Just a baby really. Little lad, two-and-a-bit years old. 'E wandered away from 'is mam. I did a spell to find 'im and it led me 'ere." He paused. "I know who took 'im", he said. "I've read 'bout 'em. Bakwas and Dzunukwa."

Richard's heart began to race. 'The toddler…that's who James is talking about', he thought.

"I'm sorry", said Maria, not meeting James' gaze. "He…he's dead. They killed him."

James clamped his hand to his mouth. "Oh no, oh God, the poor kid." A tear trickled down his cheek. He stood still for a few moments as though in shock, but then he straightened up. "'I'm not lettin' you girls die like 'e did." He inclined his head towards Richard. "This one is a werewolf, in't he? Why in't 'e changin' back into a man?" he asked.

"I don't know", replied Maria.

"We don't think he can", added Fay.

James furrowed his brow. "That's a bit weird", he said, appearing to be concentrating. "I wonder if it's 'cause of where we are."

"Yes, probably", said Maria. "Lots of strange things happen here."

"Why are we all just talking?" asked Fay. "We need to get out of here, before Bakwas and Dzunukwa get back."

The little girl's words appeared to snap James out of his reverie. "Yes, you're right", he said, looking around frantically for some way to open the cage. "There has t' be a key somewhere."

"Yes, there is", agreed Maria. "Dzunukwa keeps it in her pocket. Well…it is…it is like a pouch. A furry pouch. She carries it around her neck."

"Oh", said James. "Well, that's goin' t' be a bit awkward to get hold of. See, I 'aint really 'ere. Look." James waved his hand against the bars of the cage, and to Richard's astonishment, it passed straight through. "It's only me mind what's 'ere", explained James. "Me body is still back in't land o' the livin'. I'm meditatin' in me living' room."

Maria's shoulders slumped. "It is impossible to get out of here."

Fay began to cry. "Don't say that", she wailed.

"I'm sorry," said Maria, "but it's true".

James bit his bottom lip. "Dun't worry," he said, "there has t' be a way. I'm sure we'll figure it out."

'There won't be a way if we all just sit around here and wait for Bakwas and Dzunukwa to get back', thought Richard.

James sighed, but made no attempt to move. His expression was vacant, and Richard worried that the atmosphere of the Shroud was beginning to hypnotise him. "You know," James said, "it's getting pretty late back in't land o' the livin'. If you dun't hurry up, you won't get back before midnight."

"What happens at midnight?" asked Fay, still sniffling.

"He turns into a monster, doesn't he?" said Maria quietly.

"Well, I wun't say a monster exactly", said James, sounding

hesitant. "But aye, werewolves do change form. It's the full moon tonight, you see."

"I knew it", said Maria. "My mama used to do that too. Except she did it every night."

'I thought her mother was a witch', thought Richard, puzzled. 'And what does she mean about her mother changing form every night? That's not normal.'

"Where is your mommy?" asked Fay.

"She's...dead", said Maria, a tear trickling from her eye. "I don't really want to talk about it."

"I'm sorry", said James.

'I wonder if Bakwas or Dzunukwa killed Maria's parents', thought Richard. Then his thoughts turned to what James had just said. 'Oh hell, if I don't get out of here before midnight, I will most certainly slaughter both Maria and Fay.'

Maria stared at him straight in the eyes. "You're going to kill us, aren't you?" she asked.

Richard's stomach lurched. He whined softly. 'Not if I can help it', he thought.

It was all too much for poor Fay, and she buried her face in her hands, her little body wracked with sobs. "I just want to go home. This is a horrible place. I...w...w...w...want my m...m...m... mommy!"

"It won't surprise me if Dzunukwa gets home soon. She has been gone a while. She's probably fetching another child here for her dinner. Bakwas too, they'll both get back at some point", said Maria.

"Okay, if you girls push together wi' Richard as 'ard as you can against the gate, maybe you can get it open", suggested James. He seemed a little more alert than he had been a few minutes ago.

Richard was beginning to find it difficult to concentrate, and realised the Shroud was starting to affect him. 'This place does strange things to your mind. Stay alert', he thought, bracing himself against the cage door.

"Come on Fay, help us push", urged Maria, putting her hands on the bars alongside Richard. Still crying loudly, Fay scooted over on her bottom towards them and followed suit. "Stop crying", ordered Maria, but that only served to cause the little girl to blubber even more.

"Now look ere lass", said James. "She upset, yer great wassock."

"Wassock? Mister, you don't know what you're talking about. I've seen more children being eaten by those monsters than you can possibly imagine. This guy came to rescue us and now he's stuck in this cage, and you...I don't even know who you are. How did you get to the land of the dead anyway? Do you have magic? I used to have magic, but now I don't. I don't know why. I bet it's this place, it's all just horrible and I'm never going to leave. Even if you rescue Fay, you won't rescue me. Someone tried before but it didn't work. I'm here forever, I'm never getting out, so I'm sorry but I'm not exactly going to be lovely, cheerful and patient."

James opened his mouth, his eyes boggling, but he didn't say a word.

Richard himself was taken aback. 'Wow...kid. That's really heavy', he thought, wishing he could say something to comfort her. He didn't know what he would say even if he could talk though. The thought of how she would react finding out he was the little boy who failed to save her all those years ago filled him with trepidation.

James stared at the little girl with an anguished expression on his face. "Ee by gum lass, I wish I could 'elp, but I can't touch owt!" His gaze shifted to Richard and he wrinkled his forehead in concentration. "Werewolves can bring their 'ole bodies 'ere. They're the only ones who can, as far as I know. Do you know any other werewolves?" he asked.

"Yes, my dad", thought Richard, frustrated he couldn't convey that out loud. Instead, he nodded and whined.

"You do? Ee that's grand. I'll be able t' get a bit of 'elp then. What's your name?"

Richard rolled his eyes. 'I can't tell you my name', he thought, gritting his teeth.

"I know you can't speak", continued James. "Gotta find out your name though, 'else I won't be able t' find another werewolf. Tell you what, I'll say some letters, an' you whine when I say the right ones."

"That will take ages", said Maria. "You had better hurry up. Bakwas and Dzunukwa will be back soon."

"They can't 'urt me", said James. "I 'aint really 'ere."

"That's all very well and good for you, but they can take their bad tempers out on us", pointed out Maria. "I suppose you think they're all sunshine and smiles with us just because they can't eat us?"

James frowned. "Nay, I dun't think that", he said quietly. "Yer not stayin' 'ere. I'm gonna fetch 'elp."

Maria snorted, and Fay took her hand. "We'll get out of here", the younger girl said reassuringly.

"I've heard that before", retorted Maria.

"No time t' waste", said James, swallowing hard. He looked back to Richard. "Whine when I get the right letter. A...B...C...D..." He kept going until he reached R. As soon as he had uttered the letter, Richard whined. "Ah, your name starts wi' R? Okay, ummm... Robert? Rudolf? Randy?"

Richard remained silent.

"Royston? Ricardo?" continued James.

'For goodness sake', thought Richard. 'My name isn't particularly obscure.'

Maria stared at him. Her expression was hard to read, but finally she spoke. "Richard", she whispered.

Richard's heart sank. 'She knows', he thought. He hesitated for a moment but then whined softly, and Maria gasped.

"Oh my goodness...it's *you*", she cried.

"The name's Richard?" queried James. "'Ow do you know that?"

"You left me", said Maria, still staring at Richard and ignoring James' question completely. "You were meant to banish Bakwas and Dzunukwa, and rescue us both, but you left me behind!"

'Oh Maria, I'm so sorry', thought Richard sadly. He tried to turn his head to lick her hand as a way of apologising, but the cage was too small, and he found he couldn't reach.

"You didn't even come back for me", said Maria. "I was stuck in this cabin in the Deep Void with nobody but those two monsters for...how many years? Must be a lot because you're a grown man. I kept hoping you would find a spell to rescue me, or tell your parents, or something, but you didn't. All those years and you just forgot about me!" She began sobbing hysterically. Fay tried to hug her but Maria shook her away.

'She's right', thought Richard miserably. 'I *did* forget about her. Waking up in the hospital, being told I had been attacked by a wild animal, and that I had been dreaming. I believed them; hell I wanted to believe them, it made everything seem less scary.' He had never known such terrible guilt before. 'No wonder she's so cynical after I let her down so badly.'

"*You're* the one who she was talkin' 'bout a few minutes ago?" asked James, looking at Richard. "Damn man, you ballsed that up!" He clamped a hand over his mouth. "'Scuse my French", he muttered. "Gotta watch me language 'round kids." He sighed. "Okay, so what's 'is last name then?" he asked Maria.

"How am I supposed to know?" she replied snappily. "He was only about nine years old when I saw him last. He didn't tell me his last name. I didn't know he was a werewolf back then, and I don't think he did either. I guess that's why the berries he ate didn't do anything to him."

"Can't you tell me 'owt else 'bout 'im though?" pressed James. "I can't find 'is relatives wi' only the name Richard t' go on."

"I thought you have magic", said Maria.

"I do, but..." began James, but he stopped as a loud crashing sound from outside the cabin began to shake the walls.

"Oh no, they're back", yelped Fay.

"No more info? 'Nowt at all? I'll have to bloody improvise then", grumbled James. "I'll be back." He grinned unexpectedly. "S'good that film", he said. "Saw it wi' me wife Sarah at the flicks a few months ago."

"What's a film?" asked Maria, frowning. "What's the flicks?"

Another thud outside made Richard jump. 'Just go, James', he thought firmly. He stuck one of his forelegs through the bars of the cage at the man.

"I gotta go", said James. "I promise I'll get you all out of 'ere." With that he closed his eyes, muttered a few words, and disappeared.

"James won't return", stated Maria, her voice despondent. "*He* didn't return", she continued, prodding Richard's back, indicating she meant him.

"I don't want you to keep saying that", said Fay, beginning to cry again. "You're being mean."

The front door slammed open and in stomped Dzunukwa. Her face and hands were stained with blood; Richard could smell it was fresh. 'Human blood', he thought, realising this meant some other poor child had found themselves on the menu. A dark shadow whisked in through the door, and two red eyes began to glow from it.

'The Yee Naaldlooshii are next on my list", growled Bakwas, digging his claws into the table, and scraping them along it. 'They are making it difficult to take children. All the graves they have been digging up, making people stay home. Less children on their own to take."

Dzunukwa growled and snarled a few unintelligible words at him.

"Oh no", whispered Maria.

"What's the matter?" asked Fay.

"I think I know what he's going to do", whispered Maria, sounding fearful.

'What *is* he going to do?' thought Richard, wishing he could ask her himself.

"I've seen him do this before", she continued. "It hasn't happened for a long time though."

"What? What?" whispered Fay anxiously.

Dzunukwa growled again; she sounded agitated. Fay, Maria, and Richard, all looked towards where the ogre was stomping and roaring in the room.

"She never really likes it when he summons them", whispered Maria.

"What are you talking about?" asked Fay.

Richard had been wondering the same thing.

"It is scary", said Maria. "Really scary."

Bakwas started to become corporeal. A black skinned figure with huge talons. He closed his eyes and held his arms up in the air.

"What's he doing?" repeated Fay. Her eyes had grown large and wide and her little body started to shake.

Out of the corner of his eye, Richard could see the colour had drained from Maria's face. She put her arm around Fay as if to protect her. "You must keep your eyes closed", she said. "You don't need to see this."

As Richard watched, Bakwas began to chant. The language was strange and eerie, but Richard had heard something similar before when Pat had been reciting the magical chant earlier in the forest. It sent a shiver down his spine.

"Oh no", whispered Maria. "It is what I had feared."

Richard didn't like the sound of that. Clearly, the girl was completely spooked, and given how long she had been in this cabin, he trusted her judgement.

As the monster chanted, Richard began to get a strange sense of being watched. He became aware of an unusual wind echoing around the cabin. It didn't feel like the wind from many years ago though, this wind was very different. It had echoes of whispers floating around alongside it, as though there were spirits everywhere.

"Are those the same whispers we can hear outside?" asked Fay.

Maria nodded. "Yes," she said, "but these are very specific spirits. They are the spirits of those who have drowned."

Richard didn't know what to make of what he was hearing. 'Spirits who have drowned? I wonder why he is summoning those who have drowned in particular.'

Shadows of figures began to appear on the walls of the cabin. Little Fay gasped, and flung her arms around Richard's neck. He tried to bend his head sideways, to rub his forehead against her arm in a comforting way. 'Don't worry kid', he thought. 'I am here, I won't let anything hurt you.'

The shadows whirled around the cabin, as though they were one with the wind. The whisperings grew louder and louder, although

Richard could not make out what they were saying. Fay let out a
little scream, and buried her face into the fur on Richard's back.

"There, there", said Maria, patting Fay's shoulder. Richard could
hear in her voice she was as scared as the younger girl, but she was
clearly trying to be brave.

The shadows began almost to materialise, and Richard was able
to make out some features on them. First eyes, then noses, then
mouths. 'What the hell is happening to them?' thought Richard.
The peculiar beings snarled and bared semi-opaque fangs in their
barely-visible mouths. 'They look like Bakwas', thought Richard,
staring in horror at the shadowy monsters. The eyes of the freakish
creatures began to glow, and Richard felt his heart racing as the
terrifying red became brighter and brighter.

"Don't look at them", screamed Maria. "You mustn't let them see
you. If they notice you looking at them…just don't look at them!"

Richard closed his eyes quickly, praying the strange beings
hadn't noticed he'd been staring at them. He could feel Fay
beginning to tremble, and her arms tightened around his neck.
The wind stirred up from these creatures as they whirled around
the room, ruffling Richard's fur coat. They began to moan; low
terrible groans, making them sound as though they were in agony.
Icy shivers of fear flooded Richard's body. Involuntarily, he began
panting, his throat constricted and his mouth dry.

"Go then!" shouted Bakwas, his voice stern and commanding.

'Go where?' wondered Richard, not daring to look and see what
was happening.

At the sound of Bakwas' order, the shadowy beings began to
screech and wail. The horrible cacophony grew louder and louder,
until Richard found himself wishing he could cover his ears. The
deafening screams were so shrill, Richard was sure he was going
to be permanently deafened if it continued much longer. Suddenly,
almost as abruptly as it had started, everything fell silent. The
wind, the wailing, the groans - it all ended.

"You can look now; they've gone", whispered Maria, her voice
sounding a little shaky.

Richard was almost hesitant to open his eyes. When he did so, it took him a few seconds before he could see properly. The room was dark, and although he had heightened vision, the fact he'd been squeezing his eyes tightly shut meant he needed to readjust his sight once they were uncovered. The room was deserted apart from Richard and the girls.

CHAPTER ELEVEN

Laura felt as though she had been waiting ages for Ahiga to return, and since then her wooziness had passed. She no longer felt convinced that Richard had cheated on her, and this confused her more than ever. 'I don't understand how a memory can keep coming and going like that', she thought, quite bewildered. 'It only seems to happen when…' her gaze fell upon the bottle of liquid she had drunk earlier. 'I wonder if Ahiga has drugged me', she thought. The hairs on the back of her neck started to prickle. 'No, he's a nice guy, he wouldn't…would he?' She had heard in the news about a new drug, GHB, that had been developed as a surgical anaesthetic. Apparently there had been some recent chilling incidents concerning the drug. It had been reported that it was used in cases of date-rape. According to the reports, some women had had their drinks spiked by the stuff. 'Maybe that explains why the whiskey tasted like strawberries', she thought, her heart fluttering. 'I swear they said GHB is tasteless though', she mused. She tried her hardest to recollect anything else she had heard about the drug, but nothing else came to mind. 'Don't be ridiculous', she chided herself. 'Ahiga wouldn't do that. Anyway, I *wanted* to have sex with him.'

Laura bit her lip anxiously and sat up. 'I'd better go and find him', she thought. 'I can't stay here all night. I have to face Richard.' Her heart racing, she crept out of the tent. It was dark outside and the moon was high in the sky. 'Oh wow, it feels so late. I wonder what time it is.' She couldn't understand how it was possible so much time had elapsed. 'I must have fallen asleep', she thought, puzzled. Between the tents, she could make out a light through the trees in the distance, and the faint sound of chanting. 'What on earth is that?' she wondered. A chill ran down her spine and she shivered. The words were muffled so she crept closer, yet she still couldn't understand what was being said. The chanting was in a language she had never heard before. 'Some sort of Native American language?' she wondered. 'Could it be Navajo?' It gave her a feeling of uneasiness she couldn't shake. Gingerly, she peeked out from behind a nearby tree, wondering if she would see some sort of festival taking place. A large group of people were standing around a fire. The gathering consisted of mostly men, but Laura thought she could make out one or two women among them. Ahiga was walking around the fire holding something in his hands, lifted high above his head. 'What is that?' thought Laura, squinting to make it out. As Ahiga made his way around the circle of people, Laura gasped in horror as the object in his hands came into her view. It was a decaying corpse of a very small child, probably a baby. The rotten flesh was hanging from its face, and the stench wafted to Laura's nostrils, making her retch.

The random chanting changed to one of a distinctive recurrence of the same word, "án't'i, án't'i, án't'i." Ahiga completed his tour around the group of people and headed for the fire. Laura watched in disgust and horror as he lay the corpse on the ground before the flames, and peeled off a small section of the rancid flesh from the child, placed it in his mouth, and began to chew it.

Laura's stomach lurched. 'Oh my God', she thought, clamping her hand over her mouth. 'He's insane!' Feeling as though she would vomit at any moment, she began to back away slowly, terrified someone may hear her footsteps.

Suddenly a voice broke through the chanting. "Laura?" It was Ahiga's voice.

'Oh hell, he's spotted me', thought Laura, breaking into a run. She knew she had to get away, but it was dark and she could barely see where she was going. More through blind luck and instinct than anything else, she weaved her way between the tents and raced through the forest. The moon was full and bright, but the canopy of leaves above her head prevented the light from piercing through. Nevertheless, the little illumination present helped her to follow some semblance of path, and she prayed she was going in the right direction towards the town.

"Laura, wait!" called Ahiga, but his voice was faint and distant.

Laura ignored him and continued to hurry away from the campsite. Her heart was racing and her breath left her body in loud panting gasps. 'I must have been mad going with him', she thought, trying not to trip over anything. 'The guy is a monster!' Finally, she breathed a sigh of relief as she saw the lights of the town in the distance. The closest glow came from the lamp shining outside the little chapel within the graveyard, situated at the edge of the forest. Pushing herself forwards, she staggered in the direction of the familiar sight, then stopped briefly to catch her breath as she neared the border of the woods. She could no longer hear Ahiga's footsteps following behind her, and the sounds of chanting from the campsite had been left far behind. Something screamed in the distance and made her jump. It sounded like a woman. Then she saw, perched on a branch, an owl. 'Goddamned bird', she thought, clutching her hand to her chest. 'Scared me half to death.' With her heart thudding wildly, she began to move again, picking her way through the overgrown bushes. "Ouch!" she yelped, spiking her arm on a cluster of thorns. Flies darted around her head. She was busy wafting them away, turning and swatting at them, when she was hit by a putrid stench. She turned as a figure approached, and she let out a little shriek as the barely visible person reached out its hand in her direction. It was someone tall of a masculine appearance. "Oh my God you frightened me", she gasped. "It's very dark here, and there's all these flies. If you can just let me get past these bushes, we won't be blocking each other's path."

The figure remained silent, but took another step towards her. "Dude, can you let me get past please?" repeated Laura, the hair on the back of her neck beginning to stand on end. The stench grew stronger, and she noticed the man was surrounded by the flies. Without saying a word, the figure grabbed her arm, dragging her back into the forest. "What the hell? Get off me!" she shrieked, trying to yank her arm away. The grip around her limb was very tight though, and she felt her feet sliding involuntarily along the ground. The putrid odour emanating from this man hit the back of her throat, and made her eyes water. In desperation, she bent her head down and bit his arm. Her teeth protruded the slimy rotten flesh of the arm, as it tore away from the bone. She retched, spitting the slimy substance from her mouth. The man never flinched, he just looked down at her with eyes glowing white. Laura let out a scream of horror as she saw the rotting flesh hanging from this creature's face. She began frantically smacking the man and digging her nails into him, but it was as though he felt nothing. Laura tried to kick him, but he gave a strong pull on her arm and she lost balance, landing painfully on the ground. Even then, the man did not cease his relentless march. Laura's arm was high above her head, and the figure continued to pull her along the ground. Every rock and branch scraped across her body. She groaned in agony. "Someone help me", she managed to croak. "Help!"

Having a sudden surge of inspiration, Laura stretched as far as she could with her free hand and grabbed one of the man's legs, yanking it backwards as he lifted it to stride. He toppled over like a bowling pin, releasing Laura's arm in the process. She wasted no time, scrambled to her feet, and hurtled back in the direction of the graveyard. This time paying no attention as to whether or not the bushes were spiky, she shoved her way past them in her haste to get out of the forest. Once inside the graveyard, she kept going until she reached the entrance to the little chapel. "Please be open, please be open", she muttered under her breath. Tugging on the door handle, her heart sank as she realised the door was locked. "Shit!"

She didn't know what the terrifying figure had been. 'What does it want with me?' she thought. She turned around and froze, her back resting against the door. The graveyard, dimly illuminated by the lamp on the wall of the chapel, was no longer empty. Several people were standing there staring at her, unmoving. 'Where the hell did all these people come from?' she thought, her stomach in knots. Then she saw something that made her blood curdle. Clawing their way out of the ground, pushing up the dirt and toppling headstones over, more of these people clambered to their feet. Their skin was hanging from their faces, withered and grey. It was hard to make out in the pale light, but Laura had seen enough to realise that these were standing corpses.

Her legs nearly collapsed as they began to move towards her. She opened her mouth, trying to scream, but nothing came out. She froze to the spot, and didn't dare to even blink. 'Oh God, someone help me', she prayed, trying to will her legs into running away. Finally she summoned up the courage to move, but to her horror she realised there was nowhere to go. The group of walking bodies with glowing eyes had closed in around the chapel entrance. Every fibre of her being was telling her to get away. She desperately scanned the group in front of her, trying to judge whether or not she could dive through an opening between the advancing figures. She took a deep breath and charged straight between two of them, but it did her no good. The corpses dug their nails into her shoulders and began to pull her away from the chapel and through the graveyard.

"No! Stop! Let go!" screamed Laura, thrashing about wildly. They were too strong, and she found her feet couldn't get a grip on the ground. The rotten stench from the figures filled her nostrils once again, and she heaved, her eyes watering. The sharp corners of the gravestones cut her skin as she was carelessly bashed against them by the corpses, as they hauled her through the rows of plots and tombs towards the forest again. Her shrieks fell on deaf ears, and once again the bushes tore great gashes in her skin. She felt something wet and sticky trickling down her cheek, and she realised it was her own blood. Her face was sore and stinging but she didn't care, she just wanted to get away. She swung her head sideways against the legs of one of the corpses, hoping to knock him off-balance, but it didn't work. He looked down at her with his glowing eyes without breaking his stride. The figures seemed to know exactly where they were going despite the darkness in the forest.

Somewhere, far in the distance, Laura could hear the owl again, but this time she wasn't so sure it was an owl. 'Oh God, those really were screams I heard before', she realised. 'There must be more of these things elsewhere!' Tears flooded from her eyes, mingled with the blood on her cheeks, and met on her lips in a salty coppery union. She spat in disgust, and flung herself in all directions, trying to break free. Idle thoughts popped into her head about what these walking corpses really were, and where they were taking her. She felt as though everything she had ever known about the world had just been turned upside down. 'Maybe this is not real at all. Perhaps it's a nightmare', she thought, knowing in her heart that it wasn't. The screams grew louder. Even as she was being dragged along the bracken, her body sliding over the uneven ground, she could see out of the corner of her eye more figures, and there were petrified shrieks ringing out all around her.

BANG!

Laura gasped as a bullet flew past her head and struck one of the corpses pulling her. It went straight through the creature but nothing slowed his pace. Someone shouted something in a language she didn't understand, but she couldn't see much of anything going on. 'Is that water?' she thought, as the sound of splashing reached her ears. She didn't have time to wonder for long, for within mere seconds she found herself being shoved face-down into water. She hadn't even had time to take a breath of air first. 'Oh God I'm going to die!'

Laura tried with all her might to lift her head up, but this *thing* was holding it firmly under water. Her arms and legs were flapping erratically as she struggled to find some way to push herself up, but to no avail. She kept her mouth closed for as long as possible, but with her lungs burning and begging her to inhale, she knew she only had mere seconds. 'This is it', she thought. She had never been afraid of death before, not having given it any real consideration, but all of a sudden her inevitable demise filled her with a terror more intense than any feeling she had ever known.

Pressing her lips together so tightly she almost passed out, Laura gave one final jerk to see if she could get her head out of the water, but nothing happened. It was too much. With an almighty gasp, she inhaled a lungful of water just as the pressure on the back of her head was relieved. She felt herself being yanked roughly upwards, then everything went black.

§

The cabin seemed unnaturally still and quiet after Bakwas, Dzunukwa, and the shadowy monsters had disappeared. "Where have they gone?" whispered Fay, sitting up straight and looking around furtively.

"To the living world", replied Maria. "We have to stop them, otherwise hundreds of people will die."

"Do those scary things kill people?" asked Fay, her bottom lip trembling. "How?"

"I don't know exactly what happens", admitted Maria. "The spirits...they go back into their own dead bodies and make them move again. Then they attack people. I think they drown them. Bakwas calls them bu'kwus. He named them after himself. Last time Bakwas sent them to the real world, they killed thousands of people. I remember all the spirits of the people who had died coming into the land of the dead. There were so many, one after another. They didn't remember what had happened. I heard the whispers...they all thought they had caught some sort of disease. They were whispering about an epidemic...but it wasn't an epidemic, it was *them*, the bu'kwus."

"What's an epidemic?" said Fay softly.

"It's when a lot of people become ill from the same thing, and it spreads from person to person", said Maria.

Richard gave a whine of frustration. 'Damnit. I can't be stuck as a wolf the whole time. This is ridiculous. I need to be able to communicate with those girls', he thought.

"*We* can't stop them", said Fay. "They're really scary."

"I know", agreed Maria. "But it's awful...loads of people are going to die. Bakwas sends them when he has a reason for wanting to get rid of people. I guess he wants them to kill Yee Naaldlooshii, whatever they are, like he was talking about. They won't only kill these Yee Naaldlooshii though, they'll probably kill many more people as well. There's nothing we can do anyway, we can't get out of here."

Richard realised he knew that word. 'Yee Naaldlooshii. Skinwalkers. Bakwas is after the skinwalkers', he thought.

Fay patted Richard's head. "*He* can", she said. "He can go back to the real world if he wants." She paused and let out a sob. "He'll… have to leave us behind." The little girl sounded on the verge of dissolving into tears again.

"It's not as though he hasn't left me before", muttered Maria.

Richard's heart sank. The guilt at having left Maria when he was a boy was gnawing at his stomach, and the awful feeling that he would have to do it again was even worse. 'Fay is right', he thought. 'The only thing I can do is return to the real world and try to take down Bakwas, Dzunukwa, and those bu'kwus spirits.' He lowered his head and whined softly.

"Well go on then", said Maria.

Fay burst into tears. "I don't want him to go", she wailed.

Richard hesitated for just a moment, but he knew what he had to do. 'I'll come back, I promise', he thought, wishing he could tell them. He knew Maria wouldn't believe him though, as he had let her down so badly the first time. Not able to bear hearing the little girl's cries any longer, he closed his eyes and began to concentrate on phasing his body out of the spirit world and back into the land of the living.

"I knew he would leave", came Maria's voice. It sounded fainter, and Fay's sobs also faded until at last he couldn't hear them any longer.

The pain which seared through Richard's body the moment he re-entered the living world was so intense that at first he thought something had gone wrong and he was dying. He let out a guttural roar, half scream but half not, and dropped to the ground. It was only as the moonlight shone down through the trees, making its appearance from behind the clouds, that he realised what was happening. 'Oh God, it's the full moon', he thought in a panic. He had never before gone through the lunar change into a beast from having previously been a wolf. He had always suffered through it as a human. He had heard somewhere that it was more painful to change from wolf to beast, simply because werewolf beasts are upright and tend to move on their hind legs, unlike a wolf. Richard had never tested the theory. When human, the pain of changing was already so extreme, that he couldn't imagine it could ever be worse.

He couldn't even bring himself to howl. The next moment seemed to stretch out like an aeon of torture as his hind legs snapped back, angling themselves into what seemed like an inconceivable position. The simple action of breathing became almost impossible, as his wolf ribcage tightened around his chest, causing bone to penetrate his internal organs. Blood spewed from his mouth as he desperately tried to change back into a man in an attempt to stop this forced transformation from killing him. A burning sensation coursed through his chest, and his bones began to shift in opposing directions, some being forced by the change, others being willed by himself. Agonisingly he crawled towards a tree, pulling himself up against it as his body fought against his every action. He instantly vomited on the ground, as his torso finally shifted into a half-man half-beast state, and the bones from his elbows protruded his flesh, causing him to scream in agony as the sound of breaking bones cracked and echoed through the forest. When he looked down a second later, he could see new muscle and flesh stretching over his new protruding bones, growing to match his new form. Then his spine shifted position, arching him backwards as blood spurted from his mouth. Richard gurgled helplessly, his body convulsing. Another loud snapping noise sounded out as he tried to curl into a ball as a futile means of protecting himself from the wave of agony. Pain filled his entire body as it relentlessly continued to change against his will. His paws had become a bloody mess of exposed tendons and expanding talons. His screams became a howl, as his jaw forcefully extended from his face, tearing skin which rapidly grew back over exposed bone. As Richard's back violently snapped into position, he finally lost consciousness and succumbed to the beast.

CHAPTER TWELVE

Laura felt her shoulders being roughly shaken; she could hear a noise getting louder as she fought to understand it. "Wake up!" shouted a voice. She tried to inhale, but the fluid filling her lungs caused her to cough and splutter. Someone pulled her to a sitting position and water poured out of her mouth. She retched as she coughed up even more liquid. Her long blonde hair hung limply, wet and bedraggled at the sides of her face. Her lungs burned from the pressure of expelling so much fluid.

"What happened?" she managed to gasp. She didn't even know who she was talking to. Finally, she pried open her eyes and attempted to look about. Everything around her seemed blurry and out of focus. It was still night time, she could tell that much. The darkness felt thick and oppressive around her, like a heavy blanket.

"Those bu'kwus nearly drowned you", came the response.

Laura realised she recognised the voice that had spoken, but in her confusion she couldn't place it. "What's a bu'kwus?" she burbled. She couldn't remember what had happened at all.

"Spirits…which possess their own corpses. They try to drown people, so they will become like them", explained the other person.

Laura rubbed her eyes which stung from the water, and she stared hard at the person speaking. "Ahiga!" she exclaimed, suddenly recognising who it was. Instinctively she shuffled backwards away from him.

"Who do you think just saved you?" said Ahiga with a sarcastic tone. "We'd better not stay here because they're sure to be back soon."

"Where are they?" whispered Laura. The moon emerged once again from behind the clouds, and Ahiga was all at once bathed in its glow, which lit up the area.

"Hunting my people", said Ahiga.

"Who *are* your people?"

"Yee Naaldlooshii, skinwalkers", he replied with a smile on his face.

"What?"

Ahiga opened his mouth to reply, when suddenly an eagle's screech sounded out shrilly. Laura felt a rush of wind as it flew past her head, making her heart miss a beat. Ahiga lifted his head, an anxious expression on his face. "We need to move...now", he said firmly.

Laura staggered to her feet. "I'm not going *anywhere* with you! Thank you for saving me, but for all I know this might be all your fault. I saw what you did with that dead child at your campsite. You sick bastard. There's something seriously wrong with you. There's something seriously wrong with *all* of this. I'm going home."

Ahiga snorted. "You're going to try and run past those waking corpses to get back home to your pathetic boyfriend? You don't stand a chance."

"I'm not going with you", Laura repeated obstinately. A small furry creature brushed past her leg as it ran through the forest. She let out a yelp of surprise.

"You don't want to be here when the bu'kwus return", said Ahiga. "If you insist on running off on your own you're going to end up dead."

Laura could have sworn she saw a slight smirk on his face. "Leave me alone", she cried, thoroughly freaked out. She turned to hurry away but a chorus of screams from behind her halted her in her tracks. She swung around to see a group of about five or six people, presumably Ahiga's friends, racing through the trees towards her.

"Run!" one of them screamed. Shambling through the trees from all sides were dozens of corpses, but that wasn't what made Laura's eyes widen in horror. Directly behind the bu'kwus was a huge beast unlike anything she had ever seen before. It towered over the people in front of it, far too massive to be a bear. It was almost wolf-like in appearance, but monstrous, and standing on its hind legs. The creature's eyes glowed like fire, and even from the distance she was at, Laura could see the points of its fangs. Unable to shriek, she began to gurgle unintelligible sounds from her throat as she stared, almost frozen with fear.

"Don't just stand there! Run!" yelled Ahiga. He reached into a bag on his side and pulled out what appeared to be some type of animal skin. With a deft flick, he flung it over his shoulders, and before Laura could even react, Ahiga had gone. In his place stood a pile of clothes, and a large mountain lion.

'This is not real. This is definitely not real', Laura tried to inwardly convince herself. Sweat poured down her back. An ear-splitting roar from the huge beast made her glance over to see it bat a bu'kwus into a tree with the back of its paw-like-hand. It crouched down and swiftly bit another in half. The corpse's lower body fell to the ground, while the beast emitted a noise that sounded disgusted. The monster swung its head, letting go of the upper body with its jaws, throwing the rotten creature into the tree-line, and charged at the group of fleeing people. To Laura's surprise, some of them began throwing animal pelts or cloaks made of bird feathers around themselves, in much the same way Ahiga had done. Two changed into owls and began flapping around the great beast's head, pecking at him. The monster howled and swatted at them as though they were flies.

The bu'kwus themselves seemed to pay no attention to the beast. Laura watched as a hand reached up from beneath the soil and grabbed hold of the leg of a man who was fleeing. He fell to the ground as another corpse lurched toward him. He began to scream, kicking at the creature's hand with his other foot, trying desperately to release himself. Another arm protruded the soil, and the skeletal corpse sat up, covered in dirt. The man kicked one more time, and broke free of its grip, but the other bu'kwus grabbed hold of his hair and started to drag him in the direction of the lake. "No! No!" he shrieked, struggling, but the creature was not easy to break away from.

"Laura!" someone yelled behind her. She couldn't even turn to look around. Her legs felt like jelly and she didn't know how to make her body move.

"Laura! This way!" shouted a second voice.

'That's Pat', thought Laura. For the first time in all this chaos did she feel the smallest sensation of relief. "I'm here! Help me!" she called back.

The beast growled loudly. 'Oh crap...it heard me', she thought. Laura looked to her side but there was no sign of the mountain lion Ahiga had changed into. She took a step backwards but that just seemed to anger the beast, and it snarled menacingly at her. "Oh God", yelped Laura. She spun around and began tearing through the trees but the thunderous stomps of the huge beast behind her grew louder and faster.

"Oi! You big lug, leave 'er alone!" shouted a male voice, in a thick British accent.

Laura looked back to see the beast opening its enormous jaws, bearing fangs the size of Laura's head. She screamed as she tripped over a fallen branch, and the creature roared so loudly she was almost deafened. It brought its face down to hers as she desperately tried to back away from it. The snort from its nostrils blew her hair backwards, and she thought she might pass out from fear. "It's gonna eat me!" she screamed, her voice desperate and cracking.

A gunshot rang out, and the beast grunted and dropped to one knee. Laura shrieked as the creature swatted at her, and brought up her arms to protect herself. She felt the force of the creature's massive paw as it struck her, and she was flung across the forest ground, banging her head against a tree. She groaned and put her hand up to her hair, feeling it matted and sticky with blood from the wound.

"Are you hurt?" called Pat, hurrying over to her. A man and a woman followed closely behind, and Laura realised she had seen them before at the reservation. The image she'd had of Richard making love to this woman seemed ludicrous now, and she swallowed hard, wondering how she could have ever imagined that.

"I'll be alright", she whispered.

The beast staggered to its feet, threw back its head, and howled loudly. "Shit...where is it?" muttered the British man, fumbling in a bag on the ground.

"RUN!" screamed Laura, as the beast took a step in his direction.

Two men raced past them all, pursued by bu'kwus. They were firing out bullets haphazardly, pointing their guns behind them. Another bullet struck the beast on the shoulder, and the creature bellowed in rage.

"Stop fuckin' shootin' Richard you bloody morons!" screeched the British man.

'Richard? What the hell does he mean?' thought Laura, her head in a whirl. The beast barraged towards the fleeing men, but stopped close to where Laura was lying and turned to her.

"Go! I will hold him off!" yelled Pat, leaping up in front of Laura. The couple dragged her to her feet, and with their help she began limping away, as Pat held up his hands and began chanting in Navajo. Laura glanced back to see the beast staggering around in circles looking confused.

Laura saw one of Ahiga's men backing his way towards them. Looking around in fright, he bumped his back into a tree which caused him to yelp with fright. The man made his way around the tree, and sighed with relief as he took a step forward. Beneath his feet, two bony hands arose from the ground, grasping his ankles and pulling him down into the dirt. The man screamed as he tried to pull himself free, but in vain. Within seconds he was dragged under the surface, and water rose up out of the hole as he vanished.

"Got you, you infernal bottle", announced the British man, sounding triumphant, holding up a small vial of what appeared to be ash.

Pat was still chanting, but the look on his face was strained, as though the effort of concentration was too much for him. "We have to help him!" cried Laura, looking at the couple in desperation. The man nodded and made a move towards the beast, but suddenly a bu'kwus staggered out from behind a bush straight at Pat. Before Laura had time to react, it had flung its arms around the chanting man and instantly started to haul him away. Pat shrieked and jerked his head backwards, head-butting the animated corpse, but the creature was oblivious to the blow. The beast, no longer subdued by Pat's spell, shook its head and snarled. It reached out to swat at Pat and the bu'kwus, but someone tore through the trees and vaulted with incredible agility into the air, driving a dagger between the monster's shoulder blades.

"Kingfisher!" gasped Laura, recognising Olivia's younger brother. He was clinging onto the hilt of his blade as he hung from the beast's back.

"'Ere mate, get it to eat this stuff!" called the British man, waving the vial in the air in Kingfisher's general direction.

Kingfisher didn't respond. He just clung on as the brute swung around trying to reach over its shoulder with its claws. Kingfisher jolted about as though he were riding a bucking bronco. The beast lurched and swayed, trying to shake the teenager from its back. The woman beside Laura tore herself away from their hiding spot and ran after Pat and the two bu'kwus. As she passed the beast, it reached down and swatted at her, only missing by an inch as she flung herself forwards, falling awkwardly to the ground.

"No!" shouted the man, presumably her husband. He dived over to her side, ignoring the raging beast, only to be bowled over backwards by a group of stampeding animals; wolves, foxes, badgers, and raccoons.

"What the bloody 'ell are all those animals doing 'ere?" exclaimed the British man, looking baffled.

The beast finally managed to shake Kingfisher from his back. The young man tumbled to the ground, but landed lightly on his feet like a cat, blade in his hand, dripping with blood. The beast snarled and moved to snatch him up, but Kingfisher leapt out of the way, and sliced it across the forearm. The monster instead grabbed a fox racing past. With one swift motion the beast ripped off one of the fox's front legs. The blood-curdling screams from the animal were sickening. Laura's skin crawled as she peered through the bushes to see the reddish-brown animal change into a tall, naked man. A fox's pelt fell from his bloodied shoulders to the ground. She saw the man's eyes widening as he screamed, before the beast sank its fangs into his torso, tearing out a huge chunk of his body, causing blood to pour from his lifeless corpse.

"Oh for God's sake", exclaimed the British man, looking frustrated. To Laura's astonishment, he threw his arms up in the air, and began hopping from foot to foot. "Come an' get me then, yer great big brute", he shouted. The beast growled, turned its head towards him, and lunged, snapping its massive jaws.

'What the hell is he doing? He must be mad', thought Laura, wondering why this peculiar man appeared to be suicidal. The beast stooped to bite the British man, but as quick as a flash he stuck out his hand containing the bottle, and threw it into its mouth. The beast bit down hard, smashing the glass and swallowing the contents as it raised its claws ready to strike.

§

Richard blinked several times. It was dark and he had no idea where he was. 'What the hell is in my mouth?' he thought, running his tongue over his teeth and grimacing in disgust at the bitter taste. 'Hang on…my teeth feel weird.' He paused, wondering if he was a wolf. He could hear shouts and screams from all around him, but he couldn't tell where they were coming from. He felt lightheaded, and shook his head to clear the fuzziness. 'What happened to me?' He was confused as to why he felt far too tall. Then he glanced down and gasped at the sight of himself standing upright, but covered in fur. It didn't even sound like a gasp, but more of a growl. The realisation of what had occurred hit him like a ton of bricks. 'Oh my God…I'm…I'm…' He could barely bring himself to finish the thought. 'I'm a monster!'

It didn't make any sense. Richard scrabbled in his memories to find some reason why, or how, he could possibly be a beast, yet able to think coherently. 'Am I under a spell?' he wondered. The bitter taste still coated the inside of his mouth. 'What the hell have I just eaten?'

As screams were still filling the area around him, he felt his breath catch in his throat. 'Oh no, what have I done?' His body tensed up, wondering if he had attacked anyone while being a beast. Usually he wasn't aware of the screams, and only found out if he had caused any carnage when he regained consciousness as a man the next morning. He had never experienced self-awareness as a beast before, and it was very unnerving. Then he heard it; not just any scream, but a very particular scream. He recognised its sound. 'Laura!' he realised. He turned around and looked down at the people scuttling around. He was so tall he towered over them. At first he could only make out panic and mayhem, believing he was the cause of the commotion, but then he saw a man falling to the ground in front of him, a look of terror etched onto his face. Before Richard could see what this man was fleeing from, a hand rose up from the ground in front of the man's face, stuck its fingers in his mouth, and pulled him by the lower jaw, head first into the mud as water rose up from the hole. The man thrashed around, head held under the water. Within seconds his body stopped moving, limp and lifeless. People appeared to be terrified, but although several raced past Richard in fear, their primary concern appeared to be something else. 'What are they running away from?' he thought. 'What was that?'

Something moving in a different manner through the crowd caught his eye. Then something else - people; but they weren't running, they were steadily moving through the trees. A rancid smell of death and decay wafted up to his nostrils, and he recoiled from it. "Don't just stand there; bloody do something!" a familiar voice shouted up at him. Richard looked down to see James waving in his direction.

"What are you doing? He'll eat you! Run!" screamed another voice.

James ignored this advice and walked closer to Richard, deftly avoiding the scores of people racing around in a terrified and confused manner. "Come on, pull yerself together", he ordered. "I know this must be a bit weird, but yer can't stand there like a pillock all night."

Richard blinked at him and growled. 'What's a pillock?' he wondered.

"Richard! Yer need to…" continued James, but he never

managed to finish his sentence. Someone wrapped their arms around him, having approached from behind. "Get off me you bloody thing!" he shouted.

Flies swarmed around James' captor, and Richard suddenly realised this must be what Maria had been talking about. 'Oh shit; the bu'kwus have reanimated their own bodies', he thought. A quick glance around the forest confirmed his suspicions. They seemed to be dragging people somewhere. 'To the lake I bet', thought Richard. He lurched forward, reaching out with one massive paw and clumsily swatting at the bu'kwus dragging James away. At his stroke, both James and the animated corpse were flung into a nearby bush. James let out a scream of pain as he landed.

"My leg! My fuckin' leg!" he screeched. The bu'kwus stood up and began tugging once again at James, who emerged from the bush on his back. A stick was protruding from his ankle - blood poured from his wound onto the ground. "You could have been more careful", he wailed, reaching to up try and prise the bu'kwus' hands off him.

Richard threw back his head and howled, before thudding towards the corpse and picking it up. Unfortunately it didn't release James, resulting in him dangling in the air from the corpse's grip.

"Put me down!" screamed James, his injured leg hanging limply.

Richard took hold of James as carefully as possible with his other hand, and tried to pull him away from the bu'kwus. There was a horrible sickening crunch, and Richard's heart leapt into his throat. James began screaming with hysteria. The corpse's arm had been torn straight from its rotten corpse socket, and the dismembered body was still in Richard's right hand, while the other hand was swinging from James' shoulder, the nails digging in tightly. The one-armed corpse wriggled to try and free itself, using its own remaining arm to reach over to James, but Richard snarled at it and put James gently down on the ground without releasing the bu'kwus.

"Ta love", muttered James, prising the arm off him and pushing it away. Richard grabbed the bu'kwus' legs with his free hand and pulled hard. A river of maggots tumbled out of its middle as

Richard's force pulled it in two. Withered intestines dangled down, but to Richard's horror, the creature seemed to still be animating the body. Its eyes blinked calmly at him; Richard dropped the torso to the ground in shock, and the mangled remains of the body dug its nails into Richard's foot and tried rolling over, attempting to pull Richard in the direction of the lake.

'You have got to be kidding me', he thought, reaching down to pluck the bu'kwus into the air once again. This time he hurled it through the forest as hard and fast as he could. The foul smelling upper body, arm, and head sailed between the trees and disappeared out of view.

James tried to pick himself up from the ground but was immediately bowled straight over again by a group of various animals barraging through the forest, pursued by five or six relentless bu'kwus. 'Why are they chasing animals?' wondered Richard, but quickly understood these were not mere creatures when a snorting badger transformed into a man before his eyes. 'Skinwalkers!' he thought, his rage beginning to build up in his stomach until he could take it no longer, and he let out a roar so terrifying it shook the trees nearby. The skinwalker snatched up a long stick from the ground and charged at the nearest bu'kwus with it, running the corpse straight through the middle with a disgusting squelch. The skinwalkers stood with proud smiles on their faces for a few seconds, relishing in their triumph, before realising the creature hadn't ceased its advance.

"What the fuck is this thing?" screamed the man, turning and bolting away. A pack of five foxes raced towards the corpse with the stick through its chest. They growled and snapped at the animated corpse, surrounding it. It didn't flinch, but, to the contrary, attempted to lunge for one of the foxes, but instead found itself set upon by the entire pack. One of them clamped its teeth around the bu'kwus' leg, sinking them in deeply. A second fox leapt up and scratched the animated body across the face. None of it deterred the corpse though, and it continued to march towards the lake with the five skinwalkers in tow.

'Nothing stops these things', thought Richard in horror. 'Even biting them in half doesn't kill them.'

Another scream from the distance sounded out, and he lifted his nose to the air and sniffed hard. 'That's definitely Laura', he thought, springing into action. He took two thunderous steps when a yell from behind halted him in his tracks.

"Richard, help!"

James was wrestling a bu'kwus on the ground. Rolling around together, it was clear the bu'kwus had the upper hand. "Bloody help!" screeched James, as the corpse took hold of a handful of his hair and pulled it hard.

'I haven't got time for this, I need to get to Laura!" thought Richard in exasperation. He picked up both James and the bu'kwus, and turned to run with them, ignoring James' protests. He noticed that the foxes had torn the other corpse apart. Part of its torso was lying on the ground, the stick still visibly protruding from the chest area. One of the foxes changed back into a man, with a sort of wave-effect, similar to how Richard himself shifted between wolf and human form. The only difference was that when the naked man stood up, a fox's pelt fell from his shoulders onto the ground. He spat onto the bracken.

"That was disgusting", he announced. Richard supposed the man was referring to biting the bu'kwus. The skinwalker stopped and looked up, as though for the first time realising he was in the presence of a werewolf beast. A look of sheer terror spread across his face, and he let out a gurgling noise. The other skinwalkers, still in the guise of foxes, took one look at Richard looming over them and turned to flee. "Don't fucking leave me!" screamed the man, tearing after his comrades as they ran past two on-coming bu'kwus. One of them swiftly swung its arm down and snatched up a fox by the tail. The creature let out a loud squeal and thrashed around like a fish on the end of a line. Richard realised the position the skinwalker was in would have prevented him from shedding his fox skin and changing back into a man; instead he dangled helplessly, snarling and snapping at the corpse but unable to free himself.

Richard hesitated for a split second, feeling a fleeting dilemma about whether or not to assist the skinwalker. He knew he had to reach Laura, but something inside him was gnawing at his conscience. 'I can't just leave him', he thought, roaring with frustration. He turned back and charged at the bu'kwus; grabbing hold of its arm and ripping it off at the shoulder. The limb tumbled to the floor along with the fox, allowing the creature to change back into a man and race away through the forest screaming in terror, leaving his fox pelt behind. The one-armed corpse silently turned its attention to Richard and took a step towards him, but Richard quickly moved away and began following the scent of his fiancée through the trees towards the lake. 'Please be okay Laura', he begged silently. With his massive frame he rammed into small trees as though they weren't even there, uprooting them with ease. He didn't care; he was desperate to reach Laura. Being unable to hear her screams any longer was making his stomach churn with uneasiness.

BANG!

A sharp sting surged through Richard's arm as the bullet hit a tree ahead, and he jerked his hand upwards reflexively.

"Oww! Stop shootin' Richard!" yelled James, as his head smashed against the bu'kwus Richard was still carrying. The corpse's fingers were still clinging obstinately to James, as though it still intended to drag him away and drown him at the earliest opportunity. Its brittle skull shattered open at the force of the impact, and maggots tumbled from the gaping hole in its head onto Richard's taloned fingers. Richard balked at the stench from the corpse and the sight of the wriggling grubs. As carefully as possible, he set James and the bu'kwus on the ground close to a tree.

'Stay there a minute', he thought, hoping James would be able to prevent the bu'kwus from dragging him to the lake for at least a few minutes.

James looked bewildered, and he kicked out with his uninjured leg at the mangled corpse. "Go an' 'elp yer friends, but 'urry up would you?" panted James, wrapping his arms around the trunk of the tree and bracing himself against the corpse's ceaseless mission to pull him to his death.

Richard looked around frantically. Laura's scent had been overpowered by the odour of so many others - rotten flesh, people, skinwalkers in animal form, and even real animals who had been disturbed by all the commotion in the forest. Even with his enhanced eyesight, it was hard to see what was happening. 'Where the hell is Pat? What about the Walkers and Olivia?' he thought desperately. 'Where's Kingfisher?' In a panic, he lifted his head to howl loudly. The sound he emitted was deep, and resonated with a much lower pitched than his usual wolf cry. Upon hearing him, the screams nearby increased, and the erratic scurrying of animals and people seemed to become even more haphazard, as the sight of Richard triggered an even greater panic.

CHAPTER THIRTEEN

Laura pulled hard against the tree, her arms wrapped around the trunk. She clasped her hands together and held on with all her might. Two bu'kwus scrabbled at her legs, each trying to get a firm grasp on them as she kicked out. "Get away from me you rancid creatures!" she yelled in fear and frustration. As one lurched toward her, she lashed back with her foot, knocking it off balance, causing it to stumble backwards onto the other, sending them both tumbling into a bush. "Thank God for that!" she exclaimed. She pushed herself away from the tree and began to run in the direction she had last seen Pat. 'These goddamn corpses are everywhere. I can't take much more of this shit!' she thought, battling her way through Ahiga's men, who were either being dragged away, or being pulled under the dirt to water. She didn't feel any sympathy for them though. 'These sick bastards deserve the punishment of whatever evil they have disturbed.' She strode past a man waist deep in mud, his arms outstretched towards her.

"Help me! Please!" the man pleaded.

Laura turned to him and crouched down. "You play with matches, don't be surprised if you get burned", she said bitterly, remembering the infant's corpse they were defiling and chanting over. A withered hand rose up from the mud behind him, grabbing his hair and dragging him down.

"Please!" The man screamed, as Laura turned to walk away.

After a few steps she heard his cry turn to gurgles. Her stomach churned at the sound but she didn't look back. She wanted to get away and back to the town, leaving all the madness behind her. Pushing her way through the bushes, she tried to gather her bearings; everything looked the same. 'Hell', she thought. 'How am I supposed to find the way home?' She continued onwards, jumping at the sound of any leaves rustling in case it should be a bu'kwus. A rabbit bounded out from behind a tree, making her jump, and instinctively she began to run. She raced around a cluster of shrubs. Without looking, she bumped into the back of a corpse which was pulling someone along the ground. Letting out a yelp, she was about to race away when the person called out to her.

"Laura! Help!"

Laura stopped dead in her tracks as she recognised Pat's voice, and immediately whirled around in shock. Pat was waving one arm in her direction, desperately attempting to signal her for assistance. His face was bruised, and a cut across his forehead was bleeding. The undead creature had a firm grip of both his legs, which were raised into the air. He was trying in vain to struggle free, but being dragged on his back was obviously making it difficult for him. "Help!" he croaked again, gasping for breath.

Laura looked around, frantically searching for some way to help him. She spotted a thick long stick lying on the ground and quickly snatched it up. She charged towards the creature, stick in hand. "Get off him!" she screamed, swinging the stick around and smashing the corpse across the face as hard as she could. The bu'kwus fell to the ground, releasing Pat's legs in the process. Laura knew it would only be a matter of a few seconds though before the animated corpse was back on its feet again, so she had to act quickly. "Get up Pat, come on", she urged, taking hold of his arm and helping him up. Pat staggered to his feet and held onto her shoulder as she began to lead him away from the area. Laura hoped they would be able to put as much distance as possible between themselves and the creature.

"We have to find Olivia, Kingfisher, and the Walkers", gasped Pat. "Anything could have happened to them."

Laura gritted her teeth, torn between the desire to help and the urge to flee from the forest. Her conscience pricked at her. 'I can't leave', she realised. 'Pat's right. We have to find them.' She turned to her companion. "Water", she said. "If those *things* have taken them anywhere, we should look near water. That's where they seem to be dragging everyone away to."

"Olivia", whispered Pat. His face had drained of all colour and he clutched Laura's arm tightly. "You did not see…?" He seemed unable to finish his sentence, but Olivia knew what he meant.

"I didn't see them taking her, no, but I was somewhat distracted. Let's just see if we can find anyone."

As quietly as possible they crept in the direction of the lake, trying not to alert any nearby bu'kwus of their presence. Laura was also all too aware that there was some sort of large monster roaming around the forest as well, and the thought of coming across it again was more than terrifying. As they neared the water, the cries of the skinwalkers being forcibly taken by the walking corpses began to fill her ears. Their voices mingled together, making it difficult to distinguish one from the other. In the dark it was almost impossible to determine who was who. "Do you see Olivia or the others?" she whispered to Pat.

He shook his head, then stopped and pointed at the banking near the lake. "There!"

Laura squinted, attempting to focus in the direction in which he was pointing. Two rotting creatures were pulling someone along. At first Laura couldn't tell who it was, but when the moon's rays illuminated the person's face, she made out the features of the woman, Mrs. Walker. Her eyes were closed and Laura wasn't sure if she was alive or dead.

"Come on", said Pat urgently. "We have to stop them before they drown her!" He left their hiding place and began to race towards Mrs. Walker.

Knowing she would have to run past countless walking corpses, Laura hesitated for a second, then mustered up her courage and charged after Pat. Several of these creatures stretched out their arms to grab her as she darted through them, but each was already lumbered with a skinwalker. Pat reached the bu'kwus first. He threw himself onto the back of one of them, pulling at the corpse's arms in an attempt to get the creature to release Mrs. Walker. Laura quickly followed suit, and aimed a punch at the head of the second corpse, but in vain, for it didn't even flinch. 'It's no use, it's not working. These things are too strong', she thought, sobbing in despair. "Somebody help us!" she screamed. Her words barely formed properly for she was crying so hard. They erupted from her throat as a garbled shriek of fear, almost unintelligible.

"Bloody 'ell, I'm coming!" shouted a familiar voice.

Laura felt a wave of relief flood through her body. 'The British man', she thought. 'He'll help!'

The man ran up beside them clutching something tightly in his hands. It appeared to be a pouch of some sort, which he opened as he approached. Thrusting his hand inside, he pulled out a handful of something. Laura couldn't see what it was, until he unfolded his fingers and blew a cloud of blue powder right into the faces of the bu'kwus. Immediately they both released their grip of Mrs. Walker and fell to the ground. As Laura watched, the British man began to chant some strange words, and two ghostly figures quickly rose from the corpses. They were wispy human shapes, but horribly disfigured. Laura's eyes widened in terror as the spirits hissed, screamed, and roared. They circled her and the British man who stood back to back.

"Watch it love, these two are feisty ones", the man said, ducking as the wispy figures swooped and dived at them.

Laura peered up as one slowly approached her. She looked in amazement as it stopped in front of her. Suddenly its face turned to that of a monster, with glowing red eyes and razor teeth. It roared as it snapped at her, and she almost fainted as the British man threw more dust into the air. She held her eyes shut as they screamed and moaned. Finally peeking through slitted eyes, she saw the spirits being sucked from the air, and pulled down into the earth, seemingly banished.

"Oh my God", stammered Laura. She looked down at Mrs. Walker, unconscious on the banking of the lake. "We need to get out of here."

Pat didn't answer her. His attention was elsewhere; Laura looked around to see what he was focusing on. She gasped, her hand covering her mouth, at the sight of a horde of approaching bu'kwus. She turned to beg the British man to do something, but he was nowhere to be seen.

"Run!" yelled Pat.

Laura remained frozen to the spot, her legs trembling, unable to move. The corpses paced nearer, and she thought she was going to pass out. Black spots began to appear in front of her eyes. 'Oh no, no, this can't be how I die', she thought, willing herself to snap out of it. Something else broke through her daze however. A terrifying roar nearly deafened her, and when she blinked twice she recoiled from the wall of fur now standing between her and the horde of bu'kwus. 'The beast!' she thought, petrified. The massive creature strode forwards with determination and picked up a bu'kwus, easily tearing it in half. It lashed out at another corpse, swatting it away with such a force that its skull shattered on impact with a nearby tree. Laura barely noticed Pat beside her, tugging on her arm.

"It is Richard", he said. "Come, we must go."

His words didn't make any sense. "What's Richard? Is Richard here?" she asked.

"The beast is Richard", explained Pat, pointing to the enormous brute. "He is a werewolf. He will handle the bu'kwus, but we must go."

Laura's jaw dropped open. 'That beast is…Richard?' she thought with incredulity. 'No…it can't be…can it?' She watched as the creature tackled the crowd of corpses, its talons slashing them as they fell to the ground. "Richard?" she whispered.

The beast turned its head slightly at the sound of its name, then turned away and continued the fight. Laura wordlessly allowed Pat to lead her away from the lake, carrying Mrs. Walker between them.

§

Richard felt some relief knowing Laura, Pat and Barbara were safe, but he had no time for complacency. The relentless swarm of bu'kwus kept on attacking him. No matter how many times he knocked them down, they would get back up again. As more approached, he forced the first wave back, only to be set upon by others. Though their bodies were broken, it didn't appear to hinder their ability to launch themselves at him, and despite his strength he was beginning to tire. 'There are so many of them', he thought, frustrated by their endless resilience. Nine bu'kwus clung to his legs, weighing him down, and he struggled to lift his feet to shake them away. As he felt them climbing up his back, he thrashed and roared, but one wrapped its rotting rancid arms around his head and dug its fingers into his eyes.

Richard bellowed in pain. Encumbered by the volume of corpses swarming over his body, he lost his balance and toppled to the ground face-first. His massive form crashed hard downwards, sending a shockwave through his body. Water began to bubble up from the earth, and he tried to haul himself to his feet, but in vain. Too many bu'kwus were upon him. 'I'm a werewolf beast, this is insane, I should be stronger than this', he thought, frantically shaking his body to very little effect. The water bubbled up over his jaw and nose, and he knew he wouldn't have long before it filled his lungs entirely. 'I have to get free!' He thrashed his arms and legs but it was too late. He couldn't hold his breath any longer, and as he inhaled a lungful of liquid, everything went dark.

Richard felt his body moving, and sounds resonating from his vocal chords, yet he didn't feel at all in control. He felt nothing but pure anger. His eyes fluttered open, and he struggled to retain his own sense of self. He could feel the beast's instinctual rage bubbling to the surface. 'Oh hell, I don't want to let the beast take over', he thought, willing himself to stay focused. The fury inside him was too hard to suppress though, so instead of fighting it, he channelled himself into it, using the rage to his advantage. With strength he didn't know he had within him, not even as a beast, he thrust himself violently out of the water. Bu'kuws dropped from his body as he caught them off guard. 'I'll teach them to fuck with me', thought Richard, mentally cursing as he roared viciously and began tearing into the corpses effortlessly. He didn't know how he was able to rip through so many. His earlier fatigue was replaced with a relentless burning drive to exterminate the monstrous aberrations from the world. Scores of these creatures were ripped apart by his claws, which cut through their rotting flesh like a knife in butter.

Richard finally felt as though his efforts were paying off. Many of the corpses were now too dismembered and shattered to be able to do anything other than roll on the floor, their mouths opening and closing in a disturbing show of defiance, craning their necks still trying to reach Richard. As he continued his unceasing rampage through the horde, he caught sight of something spreading through the forest not far from where he was standing. 'Is that smoke?' he thought, breaking his concentration to peer between the trees. There was something eerily familiar about it. Two bu'kwus tried to seize the opportunity to cling to his legs, but Richard bent down and swiped them both away in one swift motion, bellowing loudly. He straightened up and stared again at the smoke-like substance. 'Fog maybe?' he wondered. Then it hit him. It was mist, and it reminded him of the land of the dead. 'Wait a minute', he thought. 'Is that…?' He gasped, which sounded more like a roar. Through the haze he caught sight of something he couldn't possibly mistake. 'It's the cabin.'

He took a step towards the building, ignoring the corpses as though they were insignificant. A glimmer of hope sparked within him. 'I can get Maria and Fay', he thought. Then a figure emerged from the front door of the cabin. A black shadowy form with flame red eyes and sharp white teeth bared in a menacing snarl, now blocked his view of the building. Compared to Richard's enormous beast form, Bakwas seemed small, but Richard knew how deadly the King of Ghosts really was. Bakwas roared in anger and charged at Richard, followed by the mist. Everything shrouded by the haze seemed only semi-real. 'He can't do anything if I get to him first', thought Richard with determination. Stomping on the bu'kwus ahead of him, Richard began to stride towards the mist. The beast's anger within his body still surged through his limbs, and he bellowed with intense aggression.

"No!" shouted a voice from behind him. "Yer great bloody fool, don't go in there! Come back!"

Richard's primary instinct was to continue moving forward,

ignoring the voice entirely.

"Stop, yer pillock!" yelled the voice again.

'There's that word again', thought Richard. 'What the hell is a pillock?' He turned to face James, who was running at him with his arms waving in the air. Richard felt a shiver of fear run through him as he looked again at Bakwas. The King of Ghosts had stopped, the mist still surrounding him, and he was snarling horribly at Richard and James.

"'E's tryin' to get yer into the mist", said James, panting as he arrived at Richard's side. "'E's tryin' to trap yer in his world again!" As James spoke, several bu'kwus sidled up close to him and grabbed hold of his arms before he could react. "Ger off!" he shouted. Richard lunged at the corpses, snatching them up in his hands and crushing them tightly in his vice-like grip. "Bloody things", muttered James. He reached into his pocket and pulled out a pouch. "This'll sort 'em out." Richard watched as his companion strode towards another advancing bu'kwus. He pulled a handful of blue powder out of the pouch and blew it at the face of the corpse. The creature fell to the ground, immobile, and a ghastly spectral form rose out of the body. Its face was hideous, and it floated around James, emitting terrifying noises, before disappearing into the ground.

"How dare you!" boomed Bakwas in a demonic voice. The King of Ghosts closed his eyes for a few seconds, chanted a few words, then started to emerge from the mist. With every step he took out of the haze, his body changed from pitch black, to more human, until finally he stood as a man. He looked exactly as he had appeared when Richard met him so many years ago, except now his long hippy-style hair was shorter and of a more modern appearance. His clothes were up to date, to match the decade. His anger betrayed him though, for his eyes still glowed with an evil red, and ugly black claws protruded from his finger-tips.

"Oh bloody hell", muttered James, backing away. He raced over to another bu'kwus and pulled out another handful of powder from the pouch.

"NO!" bellowed Bakwas. He bared his teeth in a grotesque

grimace and began to charge in James' direction, but Richard roared and positioned himself between the King of Ghosts and the British man.

A familiar voice echoed through the trees. "Richard!"

At the sound of Laura screaming his name, Richard looked to his right. Laura, and Pat had somehow found their way to him and were struggling to fend off a group of bu'kwus. Barbara appeared to be awake now, but seemed dazed, and was sitting a few feet away holding her head in her hands. Another bu'kwus advanced in her direction.

'Oh God', thought Richard. He looked at James, and then back at his fiancée. 'I have to help Laura.' Tearing himself away from James, Richard thundered across the ground to the others. He drove his talons deep into the corpse Laura had been battling against, and ripped it clean in two. Then, turning his attention to Pat, he grabbed the other creature and bit it in half, recoiling at the rancid taste.

Laura let out a scream, and Richard swung around to face her. She was pointing to James, her arm outstretched. Pat made a valiant effort to run around the outskirts of the clearing towards the British man, trying to avoid the remaining bu'kwus. Within an instant Richard charged to help James, ploughing through the corpses. Bakwas held the British man, ready to sink his teeth into his neck, his claws clasped around the man's shoulders.

"Get away from him!" yelled another voice, and Richard saw Kingfisher at a distance, running towards them as fast as he could.

Richard roared and smashed Bakwas across the face with his paw. As Bakwas fell to the ground, his hand gouged claw marks across James' chest, causing him to shriek in pain. Bakwas uttered an unintelligible cry, and from the mist his monstrous ogre of a wife emerged. She was just as hideous in this world as she had been in the land of the dead. As she made her way out of the mist, the cabin disappeared behind her as though the gateway to the land of the dead had never been there.

Bakwas screamed as Richard clamped his fangs into one of his legs and ripped it off almost effortlessly. Richard felt sick at the monstrosity of his actions, but he had no choice. 'If I don't kill him, more children will die', he told himself inwardly. 'More innocent little angels taken to be eaten, their bones tossed aside like mere garbage.'

Dzunukwa bellowed, ogre-like. Her wrinkled disfigured face contorted into an expression of pure rage. 'Oh hell', thought Richard, as Dzunukwa lunged towards him, hatred in her eyes, arms outstretched. Richard was by far the taller and stronger of them both, but Dzunukwa ploughed into him in the manner of a charging rhinoceros. Richard, momentarily caught off-balance, stumbled backwards a few steps. Bakwas immediately shot out his hand and shrieked a string of unintelligible words. Briefly Richard wondered if he was simply shouting in pain. 'Is he swearing at me?' he thought. It quickly became apparent though that this was not the case, when all the remaining bu'kwus in the area at once stopped dragging skinwalkers towards the lake, and in unison turned to stare at Richard. The eeriness of the situation made Richard's fur stand on end. Then the bu'kwus began to advance. Step after step they came, but not just the bu'kwus nearby. More and more emerged from the trees, until as far as the eye could see there was nothing but trees, and animated rotting corpses. They walked straight past Laura and the Walkers peering around from behind a bush. Mr. Walker appeared to have somehow found his way to the others, and was comforting his wife. Richard was relieved to see Olivia was with them also. The creatures didn't even pay attention to Pat on the far side of the clearing, or Kingfisher a few metres away. Instead, they made a bee-line for the huge beast.

Richard turned to face the first wave of bu'kwus as they approached him with outstretched hands. Richard roared loudly in an futile attempt to make them falter. They were thoroughly unperturbed, and continued their relentless course between the trees. They weren't even remotely afraid of him, but that didn't surprise him at all. Even through his thick fur, he could feel the sweat pouring from his brow. 'There are so many of them', he thought, wondering if his massive frame and brute strength would be enough to fend them all off. Although he had just taken on a great number of bu'kwus, this group appeared to run into the hundreds. 'Did all these people originally die by means of drowning?' he wondered, feeling overwhelmed by the sheer volume of them. He remembered what Maria had told him, that drowning victims sent to their death by bu'kwus often had their manner of demise shrouded by Bakwas in lies - stories of plagues or tragic accidents. Still, he hadn't quite appreciated the sheer quantity of how many there would be.

In his momentary lapse of concentration, Richard had forgotten everything but the bu'kuws surrounding him, so he leapt in shock as something tackled him from behind and knocked him to the ground. Whoever it was, bellowed like an angry gorilla, and Richard realised his assailant was the ape-like Dzunukwa. She sat with her full weight on his back, pinning him down for a few seconds. It didn't take long for Richard to shove himself upwards and fling the ogress from him. However that brief time allowed the bu'kwus to have made their way towards him enough that when he tried to stand back up again, their putrid bony hands reached out to grab his fur. Richard roared in anger as the creatures sank their nails into his flesh, tugging and clawing at him. At least thirty had hold of all parts of his body, and despite Richard's brawn, the spirit-possessed corpses were unexpectedly strong.

Bakwas screamed out more words Richard could not understand, and at once the bu'kwus began to try and pin Richard's head to the ground. He knew it wouldn't be long before he once again faced the bubbling muddy water which would be sure to rise up and fill his lungs. He thrashed in their grip and managed to turn his massive head to one of the bu'kwus by his shoulder. He stretched out his neck as far as possible and bit the corpse's arm in half. Quite undeterred, the creature continued to tug with its remaining arm, but suddenly someone charged out from behind a tree and ran straight into the dismembered animated body, knocking it away from Richard.

One less corpse was just what Richard needed. It gave him a tiny leeway to be able to fling himself onto his side, dislodging several other creatures. He glanced over at the corpse with the missing arm, and with a gasp saw Kingfisher lying on the ground groaning. Richard let out a howl and pulled himself upright. He shook his gargantuan body, and a multitude of bu'kwus flew from him, no longer able to cling on. Many more bu'kwus grappled at Richard, but with a roar he swung around and swiped at them with his huge arms, sending bodies tumbling to the ground. Kingfisher struggled to his knees, much to Richard's relief. The corpses still didn't pay Kingfisher any notice. 'Better they focus on me rather than him', thought Richard, knowing full well that, as a beast, he was more capable of fighting them off. Snarling and growling, he slashed his talons across the torso of an approaching creature, causing its already decaying flesh to shred into ribbons. Dzunukwa sank her teeth into his leg, but he reached down and punched her repeatedly in the head, until she slumped to the ground, unconscious.

"You abomination!" boomed Bakwas, dragging his injured body over to his wife.

James clutched his injured chest and hobbled to the nearest tree, scaling it with difficulty. Richard, briefly distracted by watching the British man struggle to pull himself up from branch to branch, let out a roar of agony as a new horde of walking corpses lunged at him, digging their bony fingers into his flesh, exposing muscles and tendons. For once he was glad of the full moon, for as a beast his body instantly regenerated and healed quickly, but the pain was still excruciating. He lashed out at them with his gargantuan paw-like hands, but once again found there were simply too many. He howled in anger and frustration as the combined weight of the corpses shoved at the front of his body. The force sent him tumbling onto his back with a crash that shook the ground like a miniature earthquake. As the creatures continued to pull and tear his flesh from him, he released an ear-splitting howl.

The bu'kwus clawed their way over his massive frame, their nails ripping into his gut in a sickening display of gore. Richard thrashed around on the ground, the pain coursing through him in waves, attempting to dislodge the animated corpses from himself. He tried calling out but the only sound which emanated from his throat was that of a monster; incomprehensible to his friends.

Through the horde of Bakwas' rotting army, he could see James up high on a tree branch directly above him. The British man pulled more blue powder from his pouch and began sprinkling it down from the tree. It rained onto the bu'kwus' heads. An intense agonising sensation from his stomach caused Richard to turn his attention back to his own body. An array of blood and a string of entrails poured from his guts. He watched in horror as several of these ungodly creatures tore into him. He felt the pain growing stronger as the bu'kwus ripped apart his insides. Everything began to appear dark around him as the torture overcame his senses, and losing consciousness, he felt a multitude of dead weights slump across his torso and legs.

Richard reopened his eyes; he realised the pain in his gut had vanished and his wounds had healed. A pile of bodies were pinning him to the ground, but he staggered to his feet, scattering them around him. A low chanting sound echoed down from the tree; he looked up and saw James performing the same banishment incantation he had cast on the bu'kwus earlier. Before Richard's eyes, the wispy disfigured forms of the spirits started to emerge from the motionless corpses. They rose into the air moaning and hissing, diving at his head as though they still intended to attack him. He ducked and swiped at them as they circled around; his claws passed through them as though they weren't even there. Then one by one they began to descend and disappeared into the ground.

A voice echoed from behind him. "Look out!"

Richard spun around at the sound of Pat's yell, just in time to see a bolt of blue light shoot from Bakwas' hands, straight towards him. Quick as a flash he flung himself to the ground, and the magical energy blast zoomed past his head and hit a tree behind him, which burst into flames. One of the branches cracked dangerously, threatening to fall. Richard looked anxiously at his friends who were inching away from the inferno, staring fearfully at Dzunukwa. She still hadn't moved, though her chest rose and fell rhythmically, dashing Richard's hopes that he might have killed her.

He grunted and tried to sit up, but found he couldn't. Something was pinning him to the ground. He turned back to look at Bakwas and spotted his lips moving. 'He's casting another spell', thought Richard in despair. None of the others seemed to have noticed; they were too distracted by the burning tree. Beads of sweat began to trickle through his fur, and he realised with a pang of worry he was rather too close to the inferno. A loud breaking noise caught his attention, and a shower of red hot ashes rained down onto his head, as a massive branch tumbled to the ground with a bang, landing right next to him. The heat made his eyes water and he could feel his fur singeing.

'Son of...' he thought, trying with all his might to get up and move away. It was hopeless. He might as well have been glued to the spot for all the good it was doing him.

"Richard get out of the way!" screamed Kingfisher, darting towards him.

"King! No! Come back!" squealed Olivia in alarm. She broke away from Pat's side and sprinted after her brother. As she passed Dzunukwa lying on the ground, she tripped over the ogress' monstrous arm and fell sprawling into the dirt. Dzunukwa stirred, and blearily pawed at the place where Olivia had landed, groaning horribly.

"Leave my wife alone you big brute!" shouted Pat. He muttered some Native American shamanistic words and held out his hands in Dzunukwa's direction. The sky rumbled for a second, then almost before Richard could react, a bolt of lightning shot down from above, aiming straight for its intended target. Unfortunately, Kingfisher had dived towards his sister to help her up, standing in the path of the lightning bolt as it passed through him, striking Dzunukwa. The electricity coursed through Kingfisher's body, lighting it up like a beacon in the dark forest. Dzunukwa gave an ape-like bellow as the lightning filled her body, causing her to spasm as the bolt drained away into the earth.

Olivia let out a shriek unlike anything Richard had ever heard before. Kingfisher's body slumped to the ground, lifeless; the smell of scorched flesh wafted from his charred body. Laura and the Walkers gasped in shock, but Pat stood still, a look of pure horror etched on his face. He seemed unable to even blink. Olivia fell onto her brother's body wailing and screaming. "Wake up King! Oh please wake up!" she sobbed, her voice shaking.

For a brief moment Bakwas lost his concentration and stopped muttering. He seemed as taken aback as everyone else. Startled, he stared over at his wife's body, which lay motionless and burned. Looking in confusion at the dead man on the ground next to her, he realised what had happened, and his eyes began to glow red with anger. "Nooooo!" he yelled through gritted teeth, raising his arms and flooding the area with mist.

Richard struggled, still pinned to the ground, as a strangely familiar blackness cast its shadow over everything. Then he saw to his left that the cabin had reappeared. As Bakwas disappeared from sight, Richard regained movement and realised where he was. 'That sneaky son of a…' he thought. 'He brought me back *here*, to *his* realm.' Clambering to his feet he surveyed the area for the King of Ghosts, but at first Bakwas was nowhere to be seen, until without warning two glowing red eyes and razor sharp teeth appeared before him. In the distance he noticed through the shadows that Pat, Olivia, the Walkers and the two charred bodies were also with them.

Bakwas turned his head to face them. "My wife is dust. I will take *all* of you for this, especially the boy; he is trapped here now. He will make a fine first meal", said Bakwas, pointing to someone standing in the shadows beside the others. Being a werewolf, Richard could make out with his supernatural sight that it was Kingfisher. The spirit of the teenager was peering down over Olivia, who was still clinging to his burned corpse, unaware of his presence.

'You will leave him alone, you bastard!' Richard thought bitterly, as he flung himself towards Bakwas, claws outstretched. He lashed out violently but his strike passed through the King of Ghosts just as it had with the bu'kwus spirits when they had emerged from the corpses. Bakwas raised his claws and swung down hard, slicing open the beast's side. Richard let out a roar, as blood began to drip from the wound, which didn't begin healing.

The King of Ghosts let out an eerie terrifying laugh. "You think you can hurt me in my own realm?" said Bakwas in a mocking tone, pointing his huge talons at Richard. He raised his hand to thrust again, but Richard tried to tackle him. As the werewolf beast approached, Bakwas bit down into his neck, causing Richard to topple to the ground as blood poured from his jugular. Unable to get back up, Richard struggled to keep himself in charge of the beast. The King of Ghosts stood over him and brandished his claws for one final strike. Richard pushed with his hands, trying to get up; as he did so, he felt a rock under his hand. Grasping it tightly he raised it up, blocking the attack. Bakwas yelled in pain as the stone hit his wrist, snapping it backwards.

Richard stared at the object in his hand. 'I'm not from the land of the dead, so I can't interact directly with him, but everything here is his own making', he realised as he jumped to his feet and slammed the rock into Bakwas' arm, causing the King of Ghosts' talons to be shoved with force through his own chest. Bakwas keeled over as they penetrated his back. Richard lifted the huge stone and brought it down hard over his opponent's head. The lifeless body slumped to the ground, and immediately the mist dissipated, and Richard found himself back in the forest. All the bu'kwus still in the area collapsed. Bakwas was no longer alive, therefore could not enable the spirits to reanimate their own dead bodies. Richard stepped back a few steps, noticing to his confusion that he didn't feel as tall as he had a few moments ago. 'Am I shrinking?' he wondered, puzzled. His wounds began to heal, and he shook his head, trying to make sense of it all. Then he realised the forest didn't seem quite as dark as it had previously; dawn was breaking.

CHAPTER FOURTEEN

Gradually, Richard's body shrank and contorted back into that of a man. Gone were the beast's massive talons and razor sharp teeth, which had been so different to his usual wolf features. Unlike the change from man to monster, the change back was not painful. It felt peculiar, not quite the same as changing into a wolf, but it didn't hurt. He felt unsteady on his human legs, and sat down heavily on the ground. He heard a thud as James dropped to the ground from the tree.

"Richard!" cried Laura, racing over to him. "Oh my God, Richard! That thing was *you*? It was true?"

Richard raised an eyebrow. "Everyone shrieking my name didn't give it away?" he asked dryly.

"No…well yes…well…I don't know. I didn't quite understand what the hell was going on", Laura admitted. "I…I feel a bit strange." She shook her head but seemed to have some difficulty focusing on him.

Richard noticed she wasn't daring to come too close to him. "I won't bite you or anything", he said.

Laura opened her mouth to respond, then looked straight past him. Her jaw dropped. Richard swung around to see what was behind him. It was hazy at first, but he saw it. The roof first, followed by the wooden walls and windows, and lastly the door. A building was materialising before his eyes.

"Bloody 'ell", gasped James, staring at the unfolding sight. "It's the cabin!"

Richard knew James was right. That was unmistakably Bakwas' cabin. No longer hidden from sight, it was solid, and right there for everyone to see. "It must not be shrouded in the land of the dead now that Bakwas and Dzunukwa are dead", he murmured.

Olivia didn't seem to notice the building, she was too consumed with the body of her fallen brother, but Pat looked up in astonishment. "This is most unexpected", he muttered, before turning his attention back to his grieving wife. With Richard's keen hearing, he could make out what Pat was murmuring into her ear. "I am so sorry. I did not mean to strike Kingfisher. Please, my darling Olivia, forgive me."

Olivia turned to Pat and buried her face against his chest, sobs wracking her body. She didn't speak, but she didn't have to; it was clear she didn't blame him for Kingfisher's death. A pang of grief welled up in Richard at the thought of his friend. 'I can't believe he's gone', he thought.

"Is Fay inside there?" asked Mr. Walker, running up to Richard. Mrs. Walker followed closely behind her husband.

Richard swallowed hard and nodded. "Yes, and another girl, Maria."

The Walkers didn't wait to hear any more, but ran straight up to the door of the cabin and flung themselves against it, half-falling into the building. Richard turned to Laura. "Umm…can I borrow your sweater?" he asked, realising he wasn't wearing any clothes.

Laura seemed dazed but she absently pulled off her sweater, revealing a blue t-shirt underneath. She handed the sweater to Richard, who hastened to tie it around his waste, preserving his modesty. "Help us!" came a shout from the cabin. His heart racing, Richard leapt to his feet. Before going to the cabin, he first ran over to Dzunukwa and wrenched the small furry pouch from around her neck. Then he tore over to the wooden building.

'Oh hell, what's happened now?' he thought. Visions of bones and half-eaten children plagued his memories, and a lump rose in his throat as he wondered what had become of Fay and Maria in the few hours he'd been apart from them. As he reached the door, Richard glanced over his shoulder to see if anyone had followed him. Pat was still comforting Olivia, who was refusing to move from her brother's body. She clung to it, weeping. Richard felt a tear trickle down his cheek as he caught another glimpse of the teenager's lifeless face.

Laura hadn't moved from her spot either. From her expression, the sheer magnitude of everything that had happened during the night had finally started to sink in. She didn't appear to be focusing on anything in particular, but sat with her shoulders slumped and the corners of her mouth downturned. Richard wanted to run back and scoop her up in his arms, but he knew his first priority had to be those two little girls. He turned away and headed into the cabin. Everything inside was the same as it had been in the land of the dead, except that in the harsh real world plane everything seemed to have a sharper edge; the haziness was gone. His gaze immediately sprang to the large cage on the far side of the room. The Walkers were tugging in desperation at the bars on the door, trying to yank it open, but to no avail. To Richard's overwhelming relief, neither Fay nor Maria appeared to be in any worse shape than they had been before. Fay had reached through the bars and was clinging to her mother's legs, sobbing pitifully.

"Get me out of here, mommy", she cried.

"Let me try", said Richard, striding over to them.

The Walkers turned to him in surprise, apparently not having heard him enter the building.

"It won't budge," said Barbara, "and we haven't the natural magic to unlock this. It must be a strong spell keeping it sealed."

Richard pulled on the bars as hard as he could, but just as it hadn't opened in the land of the dead, it didn't open now either. He rummaged in the pouch he'd taken from Dzunukwa, and extracted a long shiny silver object.

"That's the key", said Maria excitedly, her eyes lighting up.

Sticking the key in the hole, Richard turned it all the way around, but when he tugged on the cage door again it still didn't open. He furrowed his brow in confusion. "Why isn't it working?" he mused. 'What the hell else could go amiss? We're so close to getting these girls out of here, but there's something wrong with this stupid key."

"It must have a spell on it", said Maria. She slumped to the floor despondently, leaning back against the bars. "Keys are easy to get hold of, but Bakwas probably realised it was safer to use magic to protect the cage as well. Double locking system; a key and a spell."

A sound from the front door, which Richard had left ajar, caught his attention. "I'll 'av a crack at it", came a voice. It was James. "I 'aint sure I'll be able to do owt, but I'll give it a go." James closed his eyes, mumbled a few words, and pulled on the door of the cage; nothing happened. James sighed with frustration. "Dunno what else to suggest", he admitted. He kicked the floor in agitation.

"Maybe Pat can try", suggested Mr. Walker.

Richard wrinkled his nose. "I don't think he's in a position to help", he replied quietly. "He's with Olivia."

"Speak o' the devil", remarked James, as Olivia and Pat appeared in the doorway. Pat had his arm around Olivia's shoulder, and both bore red eyes, filled with tears.

"Try to free those girls", murmured Olivia, giving her husband a little push forwards.

Pat shook his head obstinately. "Look what happened when I used magic. Because of me, Kingfisher is…" he paused, his words choking in his throat. "No, I cannot. I will not use magic again."

"King would have wanted the girls to be freed", said Olivia gently. "I know my brother. He would have understood it was an accident."

"Please, please do something", sobbed Fay. "I want my mommy and daddy."

Maria put her arm around the younger girl and hugged her tightly. She looked up at Pat, her face a vision of desperation. "Please sir?" she pleaded.

Pat bit his lower lip. "I will try", he replied solemnly. Closing his eyes, he muttered a few words in Navajo. Richard felt a strange pressure building up in his ears, and it began to be painful; the same sort of feeling you get when descending in an aeroplane. Finally, just when he was sure his ear-drums were going to burst, the lock gave a loud click and cage door sprung open.

"Mommy!" shrieked Fay in delight. She tumbled out of the cage and fell into her mother's arm's, both of them crying tears of joy.

Maria emerged a little more cautiously. She gazed around the room, a look of trepidation on her face. "Have they really gone for good?" she asked, seemingly not daring to believe it.

Richard nodded. "They're dead. I wasn't going to let you spend another sixteen years with them." He paused, and dropped to one knee, looking the girl straight in the face. "I so am sorry I left you all those years ago. I had no idea things would happen that way. Can you forgive me?"

Maria looked as though she was about to respond, then burst into tears and flung her arms around his neck. "I forgive you Richard", she sobbed. "Thank you for rescuing me." She clung to him for a long time before finally standing up. She sniffed and wiped her eyes with the back of her hand. "I don't know where I'm supposed to go though", she admitted. "It feels as though I was a prisoner for such a long time."

"How long?" asked Barbara, looking across.

Maria frowned. "I don't know; I can't remember the exact date. Sixteen-something-or-other."

Richard's mouth fell open. "You've been stuck in this cabin for at least three hundred years!" he exclaimed incredulously.

It was Maria's turn to look shocked. "Is that how long it has been? My goodness…I'm so old!"

Pat stepped forwards. "I will find a suitable home for her, do not worry." He held out his hand to Maria. "Come with me, child."

Maria walked towards him and took his hand, and he gently led her out. Olivia clung to Pat's other arm, her eyes filling with tears once again. The Walkers brought Fay outside too, and the little girl blinked, dazzled by the bright daylight. James followed behind them. Richard was about to step out of the door, when Maria stopped and shook her hand out of Pat's. "Just a minute", she said. "Richard, come with me." She re-entered the building pulling Richard along with her, and scurried over to the back room. She tiptoed in, holding her finger to her lips to ensure Richard remained silent, and crept over to one of the cribs. Visibly trembling she peered over the edge, then her body relaxed. She turned to Richard. "There's nothing there", she whispered. "Would you check the other one please?"

Richard gulped, remembering the demonic children, but willed himself to walk over to the second crib and look inside. It was empty. "It's okay", he told Maria.

The girl exhaled, and without requiring any help, she shoved the first large crib out of the way, lifting up the loose floorboard beneath. "The book disappeared when you first left me", she said, glancing over at him. "This is still here though. I hid it." She stuck her hand into the hole and pulled out a green crystal. "I want you to have it", she said, handing it to Richard.

"I remember this. It's called an...emeron; that's the word", said Richard, holding out his hand for the gem. He held it up in the light and admired its sparkle. "Surely you don't want to give me this. It was your mother's, wasn't it?"

"If it weren't for you, I'd still be stuck in that cage, slaving around after Bakwas and Dzunukwa", replied Maria. "You earned it. Besides, I want a normal life. I don't want any spell-books, or strange green crystals, or anything to do with magic. I've lived here my whole life, but after what they did...I want to put all this behind me, and I never want to see this cabin again. Too many painful memories."

"Yeah, but are you sure you want to give me this?" repeated Richard, wanting to be certain. "After all, it belonged to your mom. Wouldn't you like to keep it to remind you of her? Even if you don't do magic, it would be a keepsake."

Maria gave him a wistful smile, looking suddenly wise beyond her apparent years, and Richard realised with a jolt that she had three hundred years more wisdom than he did; it was a peculiar notion to consider. "You think I need a gem to help me remember my mama?" she asked incredulously. "I haven't forgotten a single thing. I remember her hair, her clothes, her smile, the sound of her voice...everything. Her name was Tabitha." She sighed sadly. "I miss her."

Richard put his arms around the little girl and hugged her. "I'm sure you do", he murmured.

Maria returned his hug, then pulled away abruptly. "The children...where could they be? I wonder if they came back with the cabin? They could be anywhere", she said, her voice trembling as she scoured the room.

Richard ran out of the bedroom, searching in cupboards and under the table and chairs, but they were nowhere to be seen.

Maria slowly edged her way toward him. "Are they here?" she whispered, looking frightened.

Richard held her hand to help calm her nerves. "No, they must not have crossed over with the cabin. Bakwas' realm has gone. I hope for all our sakes these creatures have gone with it", he said, putting his arm around her shoulders.

"Maria, we should go and organise where you will stay tonight", called Pat from outside.

Maria pulled back from Richard and patted him on the shoulder. "I better go. I'm guessing the world is very different to the one I remember. I have a lot to get used to."

"Yeah it's probably going to be a big change", agreed Richard. He tousled her matted blonde hair. "See you around, kid."

Maria walked out of the building and Richard followed. Pat and Olivia led Maria away from the cabin. They had covered Kingfisher's body with a large sheet; Richard didn't know where they got it, but he supposed it came from inside the cabin.

"Your wife 'ant said owt to anyone. She 'int even moving now", said a quiet voice beside him. "I reckon she's gone into shock."

Richard jumped and turned to see James at the side of him. "Oh God, Laura. I forgot…" he stammered, not bothering to correct James' assumption that they were married. He didn't say anything further, but hurried in the direction James was pointing. Laura was seated on the ground around the other side of the building, away from the bodies of Kingfisher and Dzunukwa. Richard wondered if she had moved there herself, or if one of the others had led her there. Her eyes were fixed and glazed, and she didn't look as though she was capable of making cognitive decisions.

"Laura, can you hear me?" he asked tentatively as he approached his fiancée. "It's me…Richard."

Laura didn't respond, and Richard felt his own heart start to beat faster. "Laura, beautiful, it's me", he repeated with urgency.

"I'm tellin' you, she 'aint quite with it", said James, coming into view. "I reckon she needs a doctor."

"If I take her to a doctor, and she starts talking about werewolves, magic, and bu'kwus, she'll end up in a mental asylum", pointed out Richard. "Is there anything *you* can do?"

James narrowed his eyebrows. "I'm no doctor", he replied. "I s'pose I could perform a memory correction spell. If I remove her memories from the past few days, she'll have nowt to be upset about. Yer can make her believe something else happened instead."

"Wow, you can do something like that?"

James nodded. "Yep. Now go find me a rabbit. I need it for the spell; a live one please."

Wasting no time, Richard did as he was instructed. It proved easy to catch a rabbit this time as there seemed to be a great deal of wildlife activity. 'Probably due to all the bu'kwus and commotion', thought Richard. 'That's another thing though - where have all the skinwalkers disappeared to?' He snorted. "Cowards, the whole lot of them, running away like that", he muttered to himself.

James looked up as Richard approached with the rabbit cradled in his arms. "Yer got one?" he asked. Richard indicated the animal with a nod of his head.

"Give it t' me", instructed James, holding out his hands.

Richard handed James the creature. 'I wonder why so many spells seem to involve rabbits', he thought. He turned back to Laura. "Come on beautiful, say something to me. It's okay, all the scary things have gone now." He felt a little as though he was talking to a child, but still he persevered. "Let's go home and have a drink", he said. It was no use, Laura didn't even look up at him.

"I reckon I'm ready", said James after a couple of minutes. From somewhere about his person, he had managed to produce a variety of pouches, vials and bottles which he had spread out in front of him. The unfortunate rabbit was now plastered in a dark sticky-looking substance, and was squeaking in terror.

"Poor thing," remarked Richard, "is that necessary?"

James raised an eyebrow at him and gave no response. Closing his eyes, he began to mutter. The rabbit squeaked even louder and wriggled desperately, trying to escape. With one hand still clinging to the creature, James used his other hand to pick up one of the vials in front of him; it contained a yellow liquid. Still muttering, he poured the contents of the vial into a larger bottle of blue liquid. To Richard's astonishment, instead of the newly mixed substance being green, as one would expect from such a colour combination, it had become a vivid shade of purple. James stopped chanting, gave the sticky rabbit a little kiss on the forehead, and released it into the forest. He picked up the bottle of purple liquid and handed it to Richard. "She needs to drink it", he said. "As soon as she does, yer need to give 'er a new memory. Tell 'er something yer want her to remember instead o' what you want 'er to forget. She'll sleep for 'bout forty-eight hours after she drinks this stuff, an' when she wakes up, she'll believe whatever yer told 'er."

Richard bit his lip. 'That doesn't sound easy', he thought. He pondered for a moment, then nodded. "Okay", he said. While holding the bottle to Laura's lips, he tilted her head back slightly. She began to drink the liquid rapidly, soon finishing the whole lot. Richard cleared his throat. "Laura, I want you to forget everything that happened since I went to bed complaining of being unwell. This is what I want you to remember instead. I went to bed, and you joined me sometime later. The following morning I felt much better, and we both went to work. After work, we met at home, packed our bags, and went to the treehouse vacation where we spent the entire weekend having a great time. We made love, cycled, caught fish, and ate smores by the campfire. On Sunday night we came home, unpacked, and went to bed." He glanced over at James who had been listening intently, and smiled while giving him a thumbs up.

James chanted a few words to finish the spell, and at once Laura collapsed in a deep sleep. Richard had to dive to put his hand under her head before she banged it hard against the ground. "That's it then, she'll wake up Monday morning wi' new memories o' this weekend", confirmed James.

Richard breathed a sigh of relief. He tried to tell himself this was purely due to knowing Laura wouldn't be mentally scarred for life, but he couldn't deny that part of him was glad his secret was once again hidden from her. 'It's obvious she's never going to be ready to learn about werewolves', he thought. Gently letting Laura rest for a moment, he turned to James and smiled. "Thank you buddy, I couldn't have done any of this without you. It was good to meet you."

James gave him a lopsided grin. "It was nowt. If yer ever need me, seek me out."

"You know, your accent makes you sound like a pirate", said Richard with a chuckle.

James laughed. "Some folk around 'ere call me Scully Jim", he admitted. "Yanks just 'aint used to proper English."

Richard gave him a light punch on the arm. "See you around, Scully Jim", he joked. He waited until James was out of sight, then lifted up his unconscious fiancée and hoisted her over his shoulder. She didn't move a muscle. If it weren't for the fact he could hear her heart beating, and feel her shallow breath, Richard would have been quite concerned. As it was though, he trusted James. If it had not been for the unusual English man and his magic potions, things would have been a lot worse. 'He has pretty much earned my trust', decided Richard.

He traipsed between the trees for some time, leaving the cabin behind, not going too quickly as he didn't want to jolt Laura. The sun was shining through the leaves of the canopy far above, causing dappled patterns on the bracken below his feet. It seemed as though it was the start of a beautiful day; a stark contrast with the events of the previous night. The darkness and death felt a world away from the way the forest gleamed in the sunlight. Richard could always pretend none of it had happened…almost, but not quite.

A noise in the bushes caught his attention, small and almost imperceptible. An ordinary person would probably have dismissed it as nothing, but Richard's highly attuned hearing recognised that something was amiss. He turned quickly, ever alert.

"You're quick on your toes, dog", sneered a familiar voice.

"Oh, it's you", stated Richard, his heart sinking. He wasn't in the mood to deal with the skinwalker leader. "Go away."

Ahiga snarled. "Where do you think you're taking her?"

It took Richard a moment to realise Ahiga was referring to Laura. When he did, the hairs on the back of his neck began to prickle. He didn't like the skinwalker's tone. "What do you care?" asked Richard guardedly, extending his talons. He could feel the familiar tingle behind his eyes, meaning they were glowing brighter and more fire-like than usual. It happened whenever he was angry or his emotions were heightened. He growled, but Ahiga seemed quite unfazed.

"You think I'm going to let it slide that you killed Nizhoni?" asked the skinwalker.

Ahiga's words churned Richard's stomach, but he tried to remain stony faced. "I'm sure you've done worse", he retorted.

Ahiga gave a hollow laugh. "You don't know who you're pitting yourself up against", he said. "Stupid dog."

"I'm not afraid of you", said Richard through gritted teeth. "You're nothing compared with what I've just been through." He longed to change into a wolf, to intimidate his opponent properly, but he didn't dare put Laura down for fear of what Ahiga might do to her. "Leave us alone", he ordered.

"Not a chance, dog." A split second later and Ahiga had produced something dark brown and furry from the bag he wore on his back. In mere seconds, the skin was around his shoulders and Ahiga had fully transformed into a bear. His bag fell to his feet.

Richard stiffened. Even when he was in wolf form, bears were difficult to handle due to their sheer size and brute strength. He tried to avoid them when he hunted in the forest. Standing here in his human form holding Laura, he knew he would have real difficulties if Ahiga attacked him. "I don't want any trouble; just let us leave", he said nervously.

Ahiga ignored Richard's protests and began to circle him. He padded around him twice, then lurched clumsily towards him, claws extended, and swiped them across his leg. Richard grunted from the pain, his leg buckling. Still holding Laura in his arms, he struggled to retain his balance.

The bear growled and pulled itself upright onto its hind legs.

It towered over Richard, making him feel small in comparison. Unable to match the skinwalker's transformation, Richard stared in dismay at the creature in front of him. "Please go away", he tried, but Ahiga didn't seem easily deterred. Richard took a step backwards, then another, but still the bear swayed in his direction. "Oh shit", muttered Richard. Making a split second decision to get away, Richard swung around and began to race through the forest. It was easier said than done since he was carrying Laura, and although he was much faster than a regular human, Laura's weight was still slowing him down. He could hear the thudding of the bear's paws behind him, and the beating of the skinwalker's heart was never faint, suggesting Ahiga was close on his heels. Suddenly, in front of him, two squirrels dropped out of a tree, landed on the ground, and instantly turned into men. Both were Native American in appearance, in their early forties, and naked as all shape-changers are when they adopt a new form. Two tiny squirrel skins fell from their shoulders to the mud. The men scooped them up, holding them in their hands.

"You're not going anywhere", smirked one of the men. He walked towards Richard and gave him a rough shove backwards.

Richard stood his ground. "I don't know what you're trying to achieve, but you can get lost", he stated.

"Ahiga wants the woman, so hand her over", replied one of the skinwalkers.

Richard shook his head incredulously. "You're all insane." He tried to step to the side, meaning to walk around them, when something slammed into his back knocking him forwards. He realised in a split second that it was Ahiga. Richard had been unprepared for the blow, but his reflexes kicked in. Instead of dropping Laura, he managed to steady himself and dropped to one knee. The emeron tumbled out of his pocket and rolled a few feet away. Richard swore under his breath and stretched out one hand to reach it, but the bear was closer to the gem. Ahiga snatched it up into his mouth and backed away from Richard. Almost instantly, the skinwalker shook off the bear pelt and changed back into a man. He spat the emeron into his hand and held it up to peer at it.

"It can't be", he muttered, squinting. He turned his attention away from the crystal momentarily to frown at Richard. "Where did you get this?"

Richard ignored the question. "Give it back", he growled.

"I bet you don't even know what it is, dog", scoffed Ahiga in a mocking tone of voice.

Richard bristled. "It's an emeron", he retorted. Immediately he regretted that he'd revealed what the gem really was.

"So I was right then; it *is* an emeron", murmured Ahiga. "Where did you get it?" he repeated, his eyes opening wider.

'There's something about that stone he's interested in', realised Richard. 'He's trying to hide his excitement, but it's obvious.' "You and I both know I'm stronger than you", said Richard bluntly. "However I am not looking for a fight. I never meant to kill your mate in the first place. Look, if it will get you out of my life, just take the emeron and get out of here. Leave me alone; leave Laura alone."

Ahiga was once again staring at the emeron as though he were hypnotised. He didn't respond directly to Richard, but absent-mindedly gestured for his two companions to follow him. "Come now. We don't need the woman after all; we have something better", he said. The men followed him away from Richard and through the forest, in the opposite direction to the town. Richard stared after them until he could see them no longer. Then, his legs still shaking a little from the unpleasant encounter, he continued his journey home with the still unconscious Laura.

CHAPTER FIFTEEN

Richard was perched on a small wooden chair in Pat's living room. A voice echoed through the house. "Come on, hurry up", Olivia called into the bedroom.

Richard chuckled to himself. 'It's usually Olivia holding things up', he thought, amused.

"Come on!" insisted Olivia. "We'll miss her!"

"Yes, yes, I am coming", muttered Pat, poking his head around the living room door. "We can go now."

Richard followed them out of the house, through the reservation, and around to the back of the canteen. There stood a shiny new blue truck, gleaming in the sunlight. "Wow, nice wheels Pat", remarked Richard with admiration.

"Oh, I got it a few days ago", said Pat with a smile.

"He really wanted to show you, but he thought you would be busy with Laura and little Seth", said Olivia. "How are they both? Have you got used to marriage and family life yet?" She gave a wink and a grin.

Richard smiled back. He pulled a photograph of his son from his pocket and showed it to Olivia. It was a photo he had taken recently of the little boy, his jet black hair framing his chubby face. "Everything is going well, yes…" he began.

"But…?" queried Pat. He pulled open his door and climbed into the driver's side of the truck. Olivia passed the photograph back to Richard, and he stuffed it in his pocket. Then they both followed Pat into the truck.

Richard sighed as he closed the door. "I just wish I could be myself around Laura…*really* myself. We all saw the way she reacted that night in the forest though."

Olivia laid her hand gently on his arm. "That was nearly two years ago. People change. Perhaps *now* she would be more ready to learn the truth."

"No, I don't think so", said Richard doubtfully. He shook his head.

The vehicle purred to life and took off down the narrow forest trail towards the main road. None of them spoke about what had happened. Bakwas, Dzunukwa and the bu'kwus were unpleasant memories they would rather all forget about. Finally, after about an hour's drive, they pulled up outside a large mansion house. It looked dark and imposing, and the sign read *Altridge Orphanage*. Richard shuddered. "This place still gives me the creeps", he admitted.

"You know it's not so bad inside", pointed out Olivia. "It's just an old building.

They trooped out of the truck and headed up the steps to a large metal door, which was much newer than the rest of the building's stonework. Pat reached out his hand and tugged on the rope for the doorbell. At once the door flung open; a short stout lady with white hair in a bun and a beaming plump face stood in the doorway.

"Hello Mrs. Harrowgill", greeted Pat. "We are here to see Maria."

"Of course, of course", clucked the lady. "How nice to see you all again. You're just in time; she hasn't left yet. Do come in."

Richard had met this woman several times before when visiting Maria at the orphanage. It was different this time. This would be the last time they see her. They knew their way to Maria's room by heart. Down the corridor, up the stairs, take a left, down another corridor, around the corner, then it's the last door on the right. As they neared her door, Richard felt a lump welling in his throat. He had grown very fond of the girl, and he hated goodbyes. Still he knew it was in her best interests to say goodbye this time. Pat knocked on the door and they waited.

"Coming", called a familiar voice. A few seconds later, the door opened. A blonde haired pretty girl of fourteen stuck her head around the doorframe. "Richard! Pat! Olivia!" she exclaimed. She emerged into the corridor and flung her arms around them, trying to embrace all three at the same time. "I hoped you would come."

"We would not have dreamed of staying away", said Olivia, smiling.

"Are you all packed?" asked Richard.

Maria nodded. "My new parents will be here very soon", she said. She scrunched up her nose in thought. "It feels weird saying that", she admitted. "It's going to be strange, living in a new family. I've grown used to the orphanage."

"They'll give you a new start, a way to set you on the right course for the future", said Richard reassuringly.

"I know, but it's still strange. I'm not sure I'll be able to get used to calling somebody else mama."

Pat put his arm around her shoulders. "You will never forget your own mother, but this is a good opportunity", he counselled.

"I know, and they do seem like nice people", conceded Maria. "They have another girl and a boy. Apparently they're looking forward to me being their new sister."

Olivia smiled. "That sounds lovely", she said. "It will be nice for you to have siblings. You were an only child when you lived with your mother?"

"Yes, it was just mama and me", replied Maria. "I will miss you all so very much."

"We're going to miss you too kid", said Richard. He stepped back and looked at the teenager. She had changed a lot since being freed. Already she had managed to adapt to the technology of the twentieth century, and she spoke less and less of her life before being captured. He knew she would keep her past a secret from her new family.

Someone shuffled down the corridor towards them. Curious, Richard turned around to see who it was. A girl the same age as Maria, with short spiky coloured hair, was heading in their direction. She wore a studded leather outfit and looked very modern. "Mrs. Harrowgill sent me to find you, Maria", she said. "Your new parents are waiting outside."

Maria's bottom lip started to tremble, and she bit down on it. Richard put his hand on her arm to reassure her. "I will take your belongings to their car", said Pat. He held out his hand, and Maria passed him a large brown suitcase. Without a word, Pat took it, and began to walk away.

"We'll wait for you outside", said Olivia, turning to follow her husband.

When the couple had turned the corner, Maria flung her arms around the spiky-haired girl. "I'm going to miss you Carly", she sniffed, a tear beginning to trickle down her cheek. "You'll always be my best friend."

The other girl hugged her back. "You can always name your first born child after me", she said with a short laugh, wiping away a tear of her own.

"If it's a girl", pointed out Maria. "I do really like your name." She grinned and pulled away from Carly. "I suppose I had better go", she said. "I'll write to you."

"I'll write back", said Carly.

With a final hug, the girls parted ways, and Richard accompanied Maria along the corridors, down the stairs, and to the front door where they left the building. Pat and Olivia were waiting outside at the bottom of the steps. They were standing next to a brown station wagon, beside a couple in their mid forties. They both had light brown hair. The man wore a suit, and the lady wore a black and white houndstooth-patterned skirt with matching button-down jacket. They looked very smart. A girl of about thirteen with a light brown pony-tail and a boy of about five with curly mid-brown hair, were standing beside them. In her hands, the girl clasped a small figure of a white hippopotamus, decorated with flowers. She held it out shyly to Maria. "I brought this for you", she said. "It's my favourite ornament."

Maria took the hippo and examined it. "It's so beautiful", she said. "I'd be afraid I would break it." She handed it back to the younger girl. "Will you look after it for me? It would mean so much to know you are taking care of it."

The girl took back the ornament and smiled. "I'll look after it really well", she said.

"Thank you", said Maria, and gave the girl a gentle hug.

The little boy tugged on Maria's jeans. "Are you ready to go?" he asked excitedly.

Maria crouched down so she was facing him. "I'm ready", she reassured the child. "I can't wait to see our home."

Richard peered at the couple. They had genuine open expressions, and friendly faces. Richard had a good feeling about them. "Take good care of Maria", he said. "We're going to really miss her."

"We already think of her as our daughter, don't worry", said the woman. "We'll make sure she's very happy."

Maria stood up and hugged Richard, Olivia, and Pat once again in turn. "Thanks for everything, all of you", she said.

The man held open the back door of the car, and Richard's eyes welled up with tears as he pulled away to let Maria clamber inside. "Look after yourself kid", he said.

"Who you calling kid?" joked Maria. Richard smiled at the inside joke about how she was actually centuries older than him. The couple didn't appear to have realised the meaning behind her quip. Richard knew they wouldn't understand anyway.

Pat, Richard, and Olivia waved as the car drove away. Olivia was sobbing freely, but the smile on her face echoed the way Richard felt. It was better this way. Maria would have the normal life she had wanted for so long. Finally, after staring down the road for some time, even though the car was already well out of sight, Pat turned to Richard. "Will you come to the reservation for greenthread tea?" he asked.

Richard loved the traditional Native American herbal drink greenthread tea, but he shook his head. "Thank you, but no, I'm going to go and work on the cabin a little more. I've already replaced the floors", he said. "I've also nearly finished building the extension. It's hard having to sneak off and fix it up; Laura gets suspicious of where I disappear to. I don't want her seeing it; you never know, if she saw the cabin, it could bring back some unpleasant hidden memories to her. So, while I've got the opportunity, I might as well make the most of it. I'd like to pass it onto Seth when he grows older."

"I'm sure it will be lovely", said Olivia.

Richard nodded. 'The cabin really is a nice building. It's just tragic what it had been used for', he thought.

Pat smiled. "It is a fitting homage to the children who died there. The cabin is a reminder of what you put an end to", said Pat. "Come, we will head back to the forest and I will help you fix it up."

They headed back to Pat's truck, climbed in, and drove away.

About The Author

Natalie Gosney - I was born in 1983 in Paris, France in a small private clinic just off the Champs-Élysées. When I was three years old I moved to Leeds, England with my parents where I spent my childhood climbing trees, playing make-believe and reading lots of books. My passion for books only grew as I got older, and with this passion came the desire to tell stories of my own. I attended Leeds University where I studied French with Teaching English To Speakers Of Other Languages.

Later I studied Classics in addition to courses in Writing Short Stories and Creative Writing. I began my working career in 2003 at the age of 19 in a commercial estate agents which sold only *fish & chip* shops. Since then I have had various jobs, and got married in 2005. I relocated to South Yorkshire with my family in 2010. Now I am a full time writer and mother, and I wake up to the sound of cows lowing in the morning from the nearby farmer's field.

To find out more about The Wolf Born Saga™

Visit our Facebook page at:
http://www.facebook.com/WBSaga

Visit our website at:
http://www.wolfborn.co.uk

Follow us on Twitter at:
http://www.twitter.com/WolfBornSaga

This novel is the first in a series of origin books set in the world of The Wolf Born Saga™

The Wolf Born Saga™ consists of four main titles. The first being Wolf Born, the second is Wolf Witch, the third is Wolf Blade and the fourth is Wolf Bane.

Lightning Source UK Ltd.
Milton Keynes UK
UKOW04f0648200116

266731UK00001B/65/P